LAST KNOWN ADDRESS

Recent Titles by Malcolm Forsythe

THE BOOK LADY
A COUSIN REMOVED
DEATH OF A SECRETARY
FATAL REUNION
LAST KNOWN ADDRESS *
ONLY LIVING WITNESS *
WITHOUT A TRACE

* *available from Severn House*

LAST
KNOWN ADDRESS

Malcolm Forsythe

1 -3657

This first world edition published in Great Britain 2001 by
SEVERN HOUSE PUBLISHERS LTD of
9–15 High Street, Sutton, Surrey SM1 1DF.
This title first published in the USA 2001 by
SEVERN HOUSE PUBLISHERS INC of
595 Madison Avenue, New York, N.Y. 10022.

British Library Cataloguing in Publication Data

Forsythe,   Malcolm
  Last known address
  1. Millson,   Detective Chief Inspector (Fictitious character)
  2. Scobie,   Detective Sergeant   (Fictitious character)
  3. Police
  4. Detective and mystery stories
  I. Title
  823.9'14 [F]

ISBN 0-7278-5632-4

Typeset by Hewer Text Ltd.,
Edinburgh, Scotland.
Printed and bound in Great Britain by
MPG Books Ltd., Bodmin, Cornwall.

One

T he house stood on a plateau of high ground overlooking the Colne valley and Fingringhoe Nature Reserve. It was a large rectangular building – a converted eighteenth-century farmhouse – fronted by well-kept lawns and sheltered by hedges of lleylandii. At some time an annexe had been added to the side of the house and the windows there had bars across them. An asphalt drive led from the road to a large garage and continued past the front of the house and back to the road again. There was a swimming pool at the rear surrounded by an extensive patio, and beyond it a small barn that had been converted to an artist's studio. The house was called Hawkhills and some years ago, according to the Layton family, their au pair, Katrina Kovacs, had unexpectedly left one day and not been heard from again.

The house was in darkness and in the shadows at the rear of the building a dark figure crept along the patio from window to window and came to the kitchen where a vent window had been left open. The figure put a hand through, reached down to unfasten the casement window below, then opened it and climbed in.

The August night was warm and a mist from the cold river strayed across nearby fields as a black Mercedes coasted along the lane leading to the house. The man at the wheel in bow-tie and dinner jacket was Rick Layton. The fair-haired girl beside him, wearing a white evening-gown, was his cousin, Drusilla.

1

Drusilla stretched her long limbs, put a hand to her mouth and patted a yawn. 'Well, that was a boring evening,' she said. 'Yvonne and Harry seem more boring every time we see them. Did you get Harry's agreement to a merger?'

'No. He's playing hard to get. By the way, he'd like you to paint Yvonne for him. I said I'd ask you.'

Drusilla's eyebrows lifted. 'On commission?'

'Of course. But I'll pay. It'll be a present from me.'

She snorted. 'A bribe, you mean.'

'Yvonne owns half the firm, my sweet, and she knows enough about the business to realise Harry's out of touch with the latest technology. I think she'll be more amenable to a merger than he is.'

'Ah, now I see. You want me to invite her over to sit for me so you can talk her into it without Harry around?' Drusilla's lips parted in a half-smile. 'Or are you planning to seduce her into agreeing?'

'If I have to.' There was no answering smile on her cousin's face. 'Will you do it?'

'Rick, you know I only do landscapes and nudes.'

'So?'

She glanced sideways at him then exploded in laughter. 'Have that lump of lard flopped out naked on my couch?' She gurgled in her throat. 'OK, I'll do it. It might be fun.'

Approaching the house, Richard Layton slowed the Mercedes and pressed the button of a remote control. The electronic gates to the drive swung open then closed again as the car glided along the drive to the garage. As the automatic garage doors lifted and the lights came on he drove in and parked beside Drusilla's silver Porsche.

Drusilla stepped from the car, the sequins on her gown and evening bag scintillating in the light. Her blonde hair was cut in a long bob and she had hazel eyes. Her cousin had the same colour hair but his eyes were blue. They were very much alike

2

with the same full-lipped mouth, the same-shaped nose, and a confident manner bordering on arrogance. Rick was twenty-eight, his cousin twenty-six. A tall, good-looking couple.

As they left the garage and walked towards the house Drusilla gripped her cousin's arm. 'There's someone in the house,' she whispered, pointing to a ground-floor window. 'Look! In the front room.'

He saw a movement beyond the windows and started forward but she caught his arm again. 'Shouldn't we call the police?'

'By the time they get here he'll have gone. I'll deal with him myself,' Rick said in a harsh voice.

Drusilla's eyes glistened in the moonlight. 'Oh, yes Rick,' she said eagerly, relishing the prospect of an exciting end to the boring evening.

They bent low passing the windows and moved quietly to the front door. Rick opened it gently with his key and they stepped into the hall. A pair of antique duelling swords hung on the opposite wall. Rick lifted one down, its blade gleaming in the faint light from the hall windows.

Sword in hand, he approached the door to the front room and pointed to the light switches on the wall beside it. Drusilla nodded and moved forward. As he threw open the door she flicked down the switches and the room was flooded with light. Rick sprang inside, sword at the challenge.

On the far side of the room a hooded figure bending over a drawer jerked upright and turned.

'Stay where you are or I'll run you through!' Rick ordered.

The figure froze and there was a muffled sound from inside the balaclava hood. Advancing, Rick prodded the intruder towards a chair with the sword. As the hooded figure sat down, Drusilla moved quickly from the doorway to stand behind the chair.

Rick nodded to her. 'Let's have a look at him then.'

Reaching down, she yanked the woollen balaclava from the intruder's head. A mass of copper hair tumbled out over the frightened face of a young girl.

They stared at her as she sat with bowed head, hands resting on the knees of her faded blue jeans, no threat to anyone. Rick relaxed and playfully putting the tip of the sword under her chin, forced her head up. Beneath the flowing red hair was a freckled face with eyes as dark as her navy-blue sweater.

'And who the Hell are you, my pretty?' he asked.

The girl gazed back at him without answering, her eyes wary.

Drusilla gripped the girl's shoulders, digging her fingers in sharply. She was disappointed the girl wasn't the lout she'd expected to watch being given a thrashing. 'What's your name, redhead?' she snapped.

'Amy. Amy Foster.'

'How did you get in?'

'Through the kitchen window. The top was open.'

Drusilla clicked her tongue in annoyance. 'I'm forever reminding Mrs Mullins to shut all the windows before she leaves.'

Rick Layton lowered the sword and laid it across the arms of a chair. 'Where do you live?'

She hesitated. 'Nowhere.'

'Don't play smart!' Drusilla's fingers dug deeper into Amy's flesh. 'Where's your home?'

'I ain't got a home!' Amy jerked free of her grip. 'And leave me alone!' she said angrily, rubbing her bruised shoulders.

'You mean you've run away . . . left home?' Drusilla asked.

'No . . .' Again Amy hesitated, unwilling to share her story with strangers. She leaned forward, addressing Rick earnestly. 'Look, mister, I haven't taken anything. So let me go, eh?'

He ignored the appeal in the deep-blue eyes. 'Empty that haversack you're carrying.'

'I told you, I haven't taken anything!'

'Prove it then. Empty the haversack!'

Amy shrugged and stood up. Unfastening the haversack she upturned it on a table. A bundle of clothes fell out.

'Now your pockets,' he said.

She delved in her pockets and deposited their contents beside the clothes.

Rick picked up a ring. 'That's me granddad's!' Amy said sharply.

'A likely story,' he said, putting it down and picking up a wallet.

'And that's private!' she protested angrily, trying to snatch it away. 'You've no right—'

'You're the one who has no rights!' He pushed her back into the chair. 'You're a burglar . . . you broke into our house.' He opened the wallet and a folded sheet of paper fell to the floor. He picked it up and unfolded it. 'What's this?' he asked.

'That's what the undertaker says it's going to cost to bury me granddad.'

Drusilla came from behind Amy's chair and took the sheet of paper from her cousin's hand. 'You mean he's dead but not buried?' she asked incredulously.

'Yeah, well he only died last night,' Amy said.

Two

Yesterday Amy Foster and her grandfather had brought *Jonti*, the Dutch *Boeier* on which they lived at Mistley on the river Stour, down to the Colne, heading for new moorings at Rowhedge. On the way they had encountered heavy seas in The Wallet and Bert Foster had been thrown against a steel stanchion and cracked his ribs. Amy took the helm and carried on but as a consequence they were late on the tide entering the Colne. As the moorings at Rowhedge would have dried out before they reached them, they put in to Alresford Creek for the night.

While he was helping Amy to lower the heavy anchor and wrestle with the mooring chains, Bert Foster suddenly collapsed. Amy rowed him ashore in the dinghy and ran to a telephone to call an ambulance. Half an hour later they were in the Accident and Emergency Department at Colchester hospital.

As doctors attended to her granddad, a nurse took particulars from Amy. *Patient's name?* Albert Foster. *Age?* Seventy-two. 'I think,' Amy added. *Address?* 'We live on a boat.'

The nurse frowned. 'Where?'

'She's moored in Alresford Creek at the moment. We were making for Rowhedge.'

'Don't you have a home address? Parents?'

'No. There's only him and me.'

The nurse fiddled with the cap on her pen. 'So, are you his next of kin?'

'Yeah, 'course I am.'

After the formalities had been completed Amy hung around the hospital, waiting. She waited all through the night and most of the next day. Bert Foster died in the late afternoon without regaining consciousness.

Amy was stunned. Her grandfather had always been fit and seemed indestructible. She couldn't believe he was dead. 'What'd he die of?' she demanded of the doctor who told her.

The doctor looked up from his notes. 'I beg your pardon?'

'Why'd he die? He only broke his ribs.'

The doctor pushed his spectacles higher on his nose and looked at her crossly. Glancing down at the notes, he saw she was the dead man's only relative and unbent a little. 'One rib punctured his lung and he was suffering from shock and hypothermia.'

'What's hypothermia?'

'His body temperature was abnormally low. It can happen to people in shock, especially older people.'

Amy considered his words then nodded. 'What do I do now?' she asked.

'Pardon?'

'With his body. What do I do with his body?'

Observing her grim face and set mouth, the doctor had the uncomfortable thought that if the old man had died at sea she would probably have disposed of his body overboard. 'The information desk should be able to advise you,' he said.

'Right.' She stood up and turned away.

'I'm very sorry,' he said lamely.

She nodded and marched off, leaving him with the feeling he'd failed in some way.

After signing for her granddad's clothes and the possessions he had on him, Amy put his ring, wallet and loose change in her pocket and the rest in his haversack. Then, slinging the haversack over her shoulder she set off to find an undertaker.

She had no idea what coffins or funerals cost and when the undertaker told her, she was flabbergasted. The money in granddad's wallet was not nearly enough and she was uncertain how much was in the trunk aboard *Jonti* where granddad kept his savings.

'Can't you do it any cheaper?' she asked.

The undertaker looked down his nose. 'Surely you want your granddad to have a nice coffin and look his best when the family view him?'

'I'm his only family and I certainly don't want to look at his dead body,' she told him.

'I see.' The undertaker, a neatly dressed little man with dark, brushed-back hair, pursed his lips. He took a sheet of headed paper and began jotting down figures, muttering to himself as he wrote. 'Say an elm coffin . . . small hearse . . . no cars . . . meet at the cemetery . . . no headstone . . .' He finished writing, totalled the figures and handed her the piece of paper. 'That's the very lowest I can do it for – and you won't find anyone to do it for less.'

She looked at the figure. It still seemed an incredible amount to her. She just hoped granddad's savings would cover it. She nodded. 'OK.'

The undertaker reached for another sheet of paper and began taking down details from her. When he learned the body was in the hospital mortuary and Amy lived on a boat, he became doubtful. 'No family . . . no fixed address . . .' He made it sound like a crime. 'I'm afraid I'll have to ask you for a deposit – in cash.'

Amy counted out notes from the wallet and handed them to him. 'I'll have the rest by tomorrow,' she said.

'Why don't you try the Social?' the undertaker suggested as she left. 'They might help.'

Not likely. Granddad had warned her about Social Services. The 'SS' he called them because they'd tried to take her away from him and put her in care after her mum and dad died in a fire. 'Don't have nothing to do with 'em, Amy love,' he'd warned her.

From the funeral parlour Amy walked to Colchester St Botolph's and took the train back to Alresford. It was late evening when she reached the creek. There was no sign of *Jonti*.

She ran to a fisherman working on his nets. 'Where's the Dutch *Boeier* we moored here last night?'

He looked at her pityingly. 'Broke her moorings at top of the tide, lass. Drifted outta the creek on the ebb and downriver past Brightlingsea to the North Eagle. We chased after her trying to get a line aboard but she was too heavy to hold against the tide and she started sinking. Reckon some of her timbers was rotten – bin too long on the mud maybe. Anyways, she went down off the Knoll.'

Amy stared at him in disbelief. 'She can't have!' she said wildly.

' 'Fraid she did.'

Amy went numb, staring sightlessly. *Jonti* had been her home for fifteen years. Everything she and granddad had in the world was on *Jonti*. All their possessions, family records, photos, memories . . . everything. Gone. She had nothing. No granddad, no life . . . She turned away and started to run, the man's words drifting after her: '. . . claim insurance.'

There was no insurance. Granddad didn't believe in it. She ran on blindly. Along a lane, up a hill and past gravel workings with gantries standing gaunt against the twilight sky. On past chain-link fencing along the side of the road with the sheen of water beyond until she came to a warning notice: DANGER QUICKSAND KEEP OUT.

She halted, shivering. This was alien territory, unknown

and frightening with no sign of habitation. She turned away from the road and followed a bridle path to a church. When she reached the church it was a burnt-out ruin, eerie and threatening in the growing darkness. Fearful, she hurried on and came to a wood. In the cover of the trees she sank to the ground, unable to go further. Her world . . . her very existence . . . had fallen apart. She started crying in deep heaving sobs until, exhausted, she fell asleep.

When Amy awoke it was dark and the moon had risen. She sat up and forced herself to think practically. The first thing was that granddad had to be properly buried. She wouldn't let him down. She must get the money somehow, and quickly.

She stood up. The quickest way to get hold of money was to steal it. She set off to find a road and then followed it until she came to a big house without lights. It stood on its own, well back from the road. There was a nameplate on the gate: Hawkhills. She climbed over the gate and headed for the house, hugging the shadow of a tall hedge. Near the house she paused, realising that when she stepped from the darkness of the hedge her face would show clearly in the moonlight. Unfastening the haversack, she rummaged in it and found granddad's balaclava. She pulled it over her head and down over her face, adjusting it so that only her eyes showed.

In the front room of Hawkhills, Amy gave Drusilla a brief explanation. 'Granddad died in hospital and me and him lived on a boat, see. Now *Jonti's* gone . . . broke her moorings and sunk. I'd have been all right otherwise 'cos I reckon granddad had enough savings on board to pay for his funeral.'

'Why should *you* pay for your grandfather's funeral?' Drusilla asked. 'What about your family?'

'There was only me and granddad.'

The expression on Drusilla's face changed. 'You mean, you're all alone in the world? No relatives or anyone?'

' 'S right.'

'Where were you living on this boat? Around here?'

'No. Up at Mistley on the Stour. I's finished school, see, and we moved down here so's I could try for a job in Colchester.' Amy looked up. Drusilla was gazing at her intently, a strange expression in her eyes.

'Amy, did you break in here just to steal money to pay for your grandfather's funeral?'

'Yeah, o' course. Why else?' Amy's tone was truculent, as if this were self-evident. 'And for grub. I's starving.'

A smile flitted across Drusilla's face. 'How old are you, Amy?'

'Sixteen.'

Drusilla's lips parted and she let out an almost inaudible sigh. She studied Amy a moment longer then, taking her cousin's arm, she led him aside out of Amy's hearing. 'What shall we do with her, Rick?'

He shrugged. 'Doesn't seem fair to hand her over to the police. What do you suggest?'

'Let's keep her. I can make good use of her about the house and she'll be more amusing to talk to than Mrs Mullins.'

'Suppose she doesn't want to work for us?'

Drusilla smiled crookedly. 'Does she have a choice? She's nowhere to go. She's no money . . . no family . . . and we've caught her breaking in. Besides, she's desperate for money to bury her granddad.'

Rick glanced over his shoulder at Amy. 'She's very young,' he said doubtfully.

'All the easier to train.'

'A bit wild too, I'd say.'

'I'll tame her.' Drusilla moved close, and caressed the lapels of his dinner jacket. 'I want her, Rick.'

He met her eyes and smiled. 'OK, Dru.'

'Thanks.'

11

She kissed him lightly on the cheek and turned to Amy. 'We could send for the police, you know, Amy, and they'd arrest you and lock you up while they made inquiries about you.' If she expected this to frighten the girl, she was disappointed. Amy's face remained impassive.

'But we're not going to,' Drusilla went on. 'Instead, I'm going to pay for your granddad's funeral.'

Amy's eyes lit up briefly then narrowed with suspicion. 'Why 'ud you do that?'

Drusilla's slim shoulders rose and fell. 'Because I feel sorry for you and I want you to work for me.'

'Work for you? Doing what?'

'Housework. And helping in the kitchen. Can you cook?'

''Course I can!' Amy let out a snort. 'Who d'you think did the cooking on *Jonti*? Granddad didn't.'

Rick leaned forward and murmured in Drusilla's ear, 'Hardly cordon bleu, I imagine.'

'I'll teach her,' Drusilla said softly.

Amy cocked an eye at them. 'You got a room for me? I got nowhere to live.'

'You'll live here,' Drusilla told her. 'There's an annexe at the side of the house.'

'No, Dru!' Rick said sharply. He lowered his voice. 'I didn't know you meant her to live in,' he muttered.

'The girl has to live somewhere,' she said. 'It's sensible to put her in the annexe.'

'I don't like it.'

She regarded him steadily. 'Rick, it's time it was used again.' She turned to Amy. 'Come, I'll show you the flat.'

Amy followed her through a door to a dining-room and on through another door to a kitchen. It was the biggest kitchen Amy had seen. Drusilla unlocked a door and they stepped through into a small hallway. Amy wrinkled her nose at the musty smell.

'This part of the house hasn't been used for a long time,' Drusilla explained. She opened one of the three doors that led off the hall. 'This is the bedroom. The next one is a bathroom and loo, and the other is the door to the sitting-room. It'll be all yours.'

Amy stepped forward and gazed around the bedroom. She hadn't slept in a bedroom since she was a child. 'Why've the windows got bars?'

'Security. To keep out burglars like you,' Drusilla said with a smile.

Amy wondered why, in that case, there were no bars on the other windows of the house, but she made no comment. She was considering Drusilla's offer. It was a lifeline. Somewhere safe where she could get over the loss of granddad and *Jonti*. What's more, a job to go with it and a proper funeral for granddad.

Watching her face, Drusilla put an arm round her shoulder and squeezed gently. 'So, what do you say, Amy?'

Amy didn't care for a complete stranger being affectionate with her, but she didn't wriggle free. 'You'll really pay for granddad's funeral?'

'Of course,' Drusilla said impatiently. It did not occur to her that the figure quoted by the undertaker seemed like a fortune to Amy Foster.

'Yeah, OK then,' Amy said.

Two days later Amy stood alone at the foot of her grandfather's grave. The vicar stood at the head and delivered his words over the coffin as it rested on planks across the deep, narrow hole in the ground. Drusilla Layton had offered to accompany her but Amy wanted to be alone with her grief. Besides, granddad wouldn't have liked a strange woman standing there.

The undertaker's men removed the planks and lowered the coffin into the grave. As the vicar mumbled, 'Ashes to ashes, dust to dust . . .' Amy recalled a ritual she'd witnessed in the past. Stooping, she scooped up a handful of earth and threw it on to the coffin. 'Bye, granddad.'

She fought back tears. At least there were lovely flowers to lay on the grave and he'd have a nice headstone now. Drusilla had seen to all that, and arranged for a car to bring Amy to the cemetery and take her back to the house afterwards.

The service over, the vicar moved towards her, ready with words of comfort. 'That's all right. Thanks, vicar,' Amy said quickly. 'Nice service.' She ran to the car.

On the way back to Hawkhills she let the tears come. The kindly old man who'd been her constant companion since she was a child, teaching her about life and the world, was gone. She had to face life on her own now, and among strangers.

A week later, almost twelve years to the day Katrina Kovacs vanished from Hawkhills, a file arrived on DCI George Millson's desk at Colchester police station requesting an investigation into her disappearance.

Three

T he request was made in a letter from Katrina Kovacs'
father, Stefan, and the file contained reports by the
Australian police and the prison and probation authorities.
There was also a letter from a prison chaplain supporting the
request.

Stefan Kovacs had recently been granted parole, having
served fifteen years of a life sentence for murdering his wife
and her lover. His daughter, Katrina, had given evidence in
his defence at the trial and had emigrated to the UK after his
conviction to escape the publicity and harassment by the
media. For three years she had written regularly to her father
in prison and then, without explanation, her letters had
stopped and his letters to her had been returned, marked:
'Gone away. Address unknown.' Stefan Kovacs had been
held in a high security prison and his attempts from there to
discover her whereabouts, or why she'd stopped writing, had
come to nothing. Now that he was out of prison on parole he
wanted answers.

Reading the file, Millson felt empathy with Stefan Kovacs.
He'd suffered a cheating wife himself once, and lost touch
with his daughter. Much as he'd felt like it, though, he hadn't
beaten Jean or her lover to death. He'd simply divorced her
and later become reunited with his daughter.

Because of his own experience, Millson decided the request
deserved more than a routine inquiry by a DC. He thumped

on the partition wall of his office and a moment later DS Scobie's copper-coloured head came round the door. Norris Scobie, who was twenty-nine, and ten years younger than his Chief Inspector, had joined George Millson on transfer from the Met two years ago.

Millson held out the folder. 'A missing person case, Norris. An Australian au pair. She was last known to be working at a house called Hawkhills near Alresford. Have a look at the file, then call and see what they can tell you about her.'

The Amy Foster who opened the door of Hawkhills to Scobie next morning was very different to the girl who broke in there three weeks ago. Her hair had been styled and she was smartly dressed in a short black skirt and white blouse Drusilla had chosen for her.

When Drusilla realised Amy had only the clothes she was wearing she had driven her to Colchester and taken her to a smart boutique in the shopping precinct. As they were about to enter Amy pulled back.

'This place looks pricey,' she said. 'I'd like to look around for somewhere cheaper.'

'I have an account here and I'm paying, not you,' Drusilla said curtly, pushing her inside.

The manageress stepped forward and Drusilla said crisply, 'This girl hasn't a rag to her back. I want her completely kitted out. Outdoor clothes, indoor clothes, shoes . . . underwear . . . the lot.'

'Certainly, madam.' The manageress waved an assistant forward. Drusilla sat down on a nearby seat and lit a cigarette.

Moments later Amy looked askance at the armful of dresses brought by the assistant. 'I don't want no dresses,' she said.

'You'll wear what you're told, Amy,' Drusilla said firmly. She selected a dress. 'Let me see her in this one,' she instructed the assistant.

Amy resented being ordered about but kept herself in check as she was escorted to a fitting room. Drusilla had been very generous over granddad's funeral and it would be silly to cut off her nose to spite her face, as granddad himself would have said.

Outside the shop later, as assistants loaded the car with parcels and boxes, she asked Drusilla how much it had all cost.

'I have no idea,' Drusilla said.

'You should've asked.' Amy was shocked.

Drusilla laughed. 'I don't ask the price of clothes, my pet. If I want them, I buy them.' She cast a critical eye at Amy's long tresses. 'We must do something about your hair. It looks as though you've been pulled through a hedge backwards.'

She took Amy to her own hair stylist and had her locks shorn and the back of her hair razor-cut. Gazing at herself in the mirror, Amy thought she looked more like a boy than a girl.

Her first days at Hawkhills were difficult. She missed her grandfather and found it hard to adjust to living in a house after years of living afloat. Also, there were things like microwave ovens, dishwashers and washing machines to learn about.

'You mean you've never even used a vacuum cleaner before?' Drusilla's eyebrows lifted in amazement.

'Weren't no call for one on *Jonti*,' Amy said.

'How long had you lived on a boat, Amy?'

'Since I was 'bout four.'

'What happened to your parents?'

'They died in a fire. There weren't no one else to look after me 'cept granddad, so I went and lived with him on his boat.'

'How did you manage for money?'

'Granddad had his pension and he made a good living tending lobster pots in Pennyhole Bay. He was good with his hands too. Made furniture, he did, and lovely model ships. Got good money for everything too.'

Early on, Amy asked whether she should call her Miss Layton or Madam.

'Neither,' Drusilla said. 'Drusilla will do fine.'

Amy was doubtful. 'Even in front of other people?'

Drusilla smiled. 'No, then it had better be Miss Layton,' she said.

So, when Scobie showed his warrant card and asked to speak to Mrs Layton, Amy made him repeat himself and then told him, 'There's no *Mrs* Layton here, only *Miss* Layton.'

'I expect she'll do,' said Scobie.

'Miss Layton's in her studio,' Amy said. She lifted a handset beside the door, pressed a button and spoke into it. She hung up. 'I'm to take you down there,' she said. 'This way.'

Scobie followed her across the hall, through a sitting-room and out through French windows. 'Who else lives here?' he asked, as they made a circuit of the swimming pool and took a path across the lawn.

'Only Miss Drusilla's cousin, Mr Rick.' Amy skirted a small pond. 'And me o'course, Amy Foster.'

'How long have you worked here, Amy?'

Amy stopped. Years ago, a policeman had helped a social worker drag her away from granddad, screaming and shouting. She'd been four years old. Granddad had gone straight to a solicitor who'd applied to a judge-in-chambers and got her back again the next day. But she and granddad had never trusted policemen since. 'Why d'you want to know?' she asked.

'Just curious,' Scobie told her.

'Curiosity killed the cat,' Amy said, walking on quickly towards a barn and forcing him to take long strides to keep up with her. She paused at a door in the side of the barn then knocked and entered. 'Detective Sergeant Scobie, Miss Layton,' she announced, and stood aside for him to enter.

Scobie stepped inside. It seemed almost lighter inside the building than out. One side of the barn had been replaced by glass and there were large skylights in the roof. Glancing around he saw canvases and sketches in various stages of completion propped against the walls. There were also finished ones, some framed, some unframed.

Drusilla Layton, in smock and trousers, was standing at an easel with her back to him. She had a brush in her hand and another between her teeth. Without turning round she removed the brush from between her teeth with her free hand and asked brusquely, 'What do you want, Sergeant?'

'I'm making inquiries about a Katrina Kovacs. I understand she once worked here.'

For a moment Drusilla went on painting. Then she carefully put the brushes down on the table beside her, wiped her fingers on her smock and turned round. Scobie took in the wide-apart blue eyes and long, narrow face with pointed chin and nose. A striking face, beautiful but not pretty, he decided.

'That was years ago,' she said. 'Why are you asking about her after all this time?'

'Her father wants to find her.'

Her eyebrows lifted. 'I didn't know she had a father. She never mentioned him.'

'That was probably because he was in prison.'

'Really? How interesting. What for?'

'He murdered her mother,' Scobie said bluntly, expecting to puncture Drusilla Layton's offhand manner, which was beginning to annoy him. But all she said was, 'Poor Katrina.'

He went on, 'This is her last known address and he hasn't heard from her since she left.'

'Well, no one here can help you, Sergeant. Katrina just

upped and went one day. Took all her things and never even said goodbye. No one knew why.'

'You could only have been a child then, Miss Layton,' Scobie said irritably. 'I'd like to speak to your mother and father. I gather they don't live here, so where can I find them?'

'Mother's moved out, father's dead,' she said laconically. 'I'll give you her address.' She turned away to the table, scribbled on a pad and tore the sheet off. 'It's not far away,' she said, handing it to him.

'Thank you. Was anyone else living here when Katrina left?'

'No. Granny was staying with us but she's bonkers now and we've put her in Ridgewell. It's a sort of rest home – a secure one.'

'I see. Well, I won't take any more of your time, Miss Layton.'

She nodded. 'Amy will see you out.' She turned back to her easel and picked up the brushes.

Amy materialised from behind him. As Scobie turned to follow her he came face to face with a pastel sketch leaning against the wall. It was a life-sized portrait of Amy Foster lying on a couch. She was completely nude.

Drusilla's mother, Constance, lived in a thatched cottage near Little Bentley. As Scobie opened the gate to walk up the path, a pair of German shepherd dogs came bounding towards him, barking loudly. He halted and stood stock still, relieved to see them stop and lie down a few yards from him, alert and watchful. A woman in corduroys and white shirt appeared at the front door.

'Mrs Layton?' Scobie called. She nodded. 'Detective Sergeant Scobie. May I have a word?'

'Yes, come in. *Stay! Sit!*' she commanded, as the dogs came to their feet. They sat.

'They're very well trained,' Scobie said, stepping warily between them as he walked forward.

'So they should be. Romulus and Remus are retired RAF guard dogs,' she said, smiling. 'They belonged to my mother. When she had to go into care, I couldn't bear to have them put down, so I kept them with me.'

Close to, Constance Layton looked to be in her late forties. She had the same blonde hair and striking face as her daughter, but Scobie thought she seemed more friendly.

As they sat down in the front room she said, 'I'd no idea Katrina's father was a murderer,' and Scobie realised Drusilla had already phoned and warned her of his visit. 'That must be why she was so secretive and we knew so little about her,' she added, looking him straight in the face.

Scobie wondered if she would make this her excuse for not answering some of his questions about the girl. 'How long did Katrina work for you?' he asked.

'About three years.'

'And I understand from your daughter she left without giving any explanation.'

'That's right, and it was most inconvenient,' Constance Layton said. 'My mother was staying at Hawkhills then and we had Drusilla's cousin, Richard, with us for the school holidays.'

'When was this exactly?'

'The week before the children went back to school. That would make it the second week in September, twelve years ago.'

'And can you remember what happened the day she left?'

'Oh yes, I can remember very well. Katrina was on her own in the house. I'd taken the children to the beach for the day, and my mother had gone to her own place to collect some things. My husband was working abroad then. As my mother was returning, she saw Katrina and a man putting suitcases

21

into a taxi. Before she could reach the front door to ask Katrina what she was doing, the taxi drove off.'

'She didn't leave a note or anything?'

'Absolutely nothing. We waited a week or so, expecting her to phone, and when she didn't I notified the police.'

'Why did you do that?'

'Well . . .' She hesitated, seeming to be taken aback by the question. 'Well, I had responsibility for her as she was under my roof as an au pair. Besides, she was Australian and a stranger to the country.'

'Did they take any action?'

'Not really, although a constable called and interviewed mother and me. He said unless a crime had been committed, or there was reason to believe Katrina was in danger, she was not their concern.'

Scobie nodded. 'And you never heard from her again?'

'Not a word. One or two letters came for her after she left. I wrote "Gone away" on them and put them back in the post.'

'Do you know of any reason for her to leave like that, Mrs Layton?'

'No, at least not at the time. It seems obvious now though, knowing about her father. She must have met up with this man – the man who was with her in the taxi – and decided to go off with him. As I said, she was very secretive. She didn't tell us where she went on her days off, or who she met. Perhaps she saw this man as her chance to start a new life and make a break with the past. It's the most likely explanation, don't you think, Sergeant?' She gazed at him earnestly.

'It's certainly a possibility,' Scobie said cautiously. He closed his notebook. 'Well, thank you, Mrs Layton. I don't need to bother you any further.'

At the door she said, 'I do hope you won't find it necessary to worry my mother, Sergeant. She's in a home and she's very old and not at all well. She wouldn't be able to tell you any more than she told the police at the time.'

'I see no reason to trouble your mother,' Scobie assured her.

'Good. I'm so glad.' She held out her hand.

On his return to the office Scobie searched the divisional records for a note of the previous inquiry, not expecting to find one on such a trivial matter. However, the DC who visited Mrs Layton twelve years ago had dutifully filed a report and it had been retained in archives. It confirmed what Constance Layton had told Scobie. Her mother, Julia Dean, had seen Katrina, with her suitcase and accompanied by a man, leave Hawkhills in a taxi. Katrina had gone willingly and seemed on friendly terms with the man. Both women said they knew of no reason for Katrina to leave unexpectedly, and they had no idea who the man was. The report had been logged, marked 'No further action' and filed.

When he reported his interview with Constance Layton to Millson, Scobie expressed a similar opinion. 'The most likely explanation of her leaving is she'd met a man and taken the opportunity to break with her father. After all,' he added, 'he did murder her mother. There's no need for us to take this further, I think.'

'That's your considered view, is it, Norris? She's the way-ward daughter of a man who killed his cheating wife and so we don't waste any more time on her?' Millson's tone was brittle.

'Well, that wasn't what I—'

'Stefan Kovacs gets the same help as any other man searching for his missing daughter. We do our best to find her. Understood?'

'Understood,' Scobie said, aggrieved by the criticism. He knew Millson was over-sensitive on the subject of fathers parted from daughters, but he thought his concern was unjustified in this case.

'You should have questioned Mrs Layton harder, Norris,' Millson said in a milder tone. 'The girl lived with the family for three years. Don't tell me they know nothing about her. The first thing, though, is to try and trace that taxi driver and make inquiries in Alresford to see if anyone remembers Katrina.'

'It would help if we had a photo of her,' Scobie said.

'I know.' Millson nodded. 'I've already asked for photographs, letters and any other information the father might have.'

Four

The following morning Yvonne Weston drove over from Kelvedon for her first sitting with Drusilla. She was excited at the prospect of having her portrait painted. It would be something to tell her friends about. Her long dark hair had been restyled and she'd bought a new dress for the occasion. The dress was royal blue and had a mandarin collar that made her look regal. Around her neck she wore a gold chain given to her by her father.

Yvonne was forty-one. Her husband, Harry, was forty-two, a heavy man with thin, sandy hair and a ginger moustache. He managed a data-processing installation near the Albert Embankment in London which processed payrolls and accounts for small firms unable, or unwilling, to face the problems and expense of setting up a computer facility of their own. The installation had been set up with a loan from Yvonne's father and it had always irked Harry that Yvonne had a father with money. His own father had died when Harry was three, leaving his mother nothing but debts.

Yvonne had been married to Harry Weston for fifteen years and she was discontented and bored with her life. She thought Drusilla and Rick Layton were daring and modern and wished she and Harry could meet more people like them.

The gate to the drive at Hawkhills was closed when she arrived. Leaning out of her car window she pressed the buzzer beside the gate and spoke into the microphone. A girl's voice

25

answered and the gate swung open. Yvonne drove slowly up the drive, admiring the house and its setting. It had always been dark the evenings she and Harry came to dinner and she hadn't realised the extent of the grounds. Their own house at Kelvedon was modern. It was detached – just – separated from neighbouring houses by a narrow gap on one side and adjoining garages on the other.

She remembered Hawkhills as being rather grand inside with hanging paintings, Georgian furniture and Inglenook fireplaces. Everything was in keeping and discreetly valuable, unlike Harry's vulgar, gold-plated taps and lacquered brass door furniture. It was not simply a matter of having a Steinway grand, or a maid to answer the door like the Laytons, though, Yvonne thought. You had to have the background and upbringing to go with it.

Drusilla greeted her in the lounge wearing a white shirt over grey trousers. 'Shall we start right away, or would you like a drink or something first?' she asked.

'Oh, I'm ready to start at once,' Yvonne said eagerly.

'OK then. Studio's this way.' Drusilla opened the French windows and stepped on to the patio.

'Have you always lived at Hawkhills?' Yvonne asked as she followed her.

'Yes, we have. Rick and I were born here.'

They reached the studio and Drusilla opened the door. 'Just pop behind the screen and slip your clothes off, Yvonne,' she said as they entered.

Startled, Yvonne stopped. 'You're not going to paint me in the nude, are you?'

'Of course. You're not shy, are you?' Drusilla's voice was faintly mocking.

'No-um . . . it's just that . . . well, I wasn't expecting it.' She was sure Harry wasn't either and she wondered what his reaction would be.

'Everything?' she called over the screen a few moments later, hoping she might be allowed to retain at least some small covering. Yvonne Weston was not proud of her figure and she was reluctant to reveal it to the slender Drusilla.

'Everything. If you feel cold I can switch a heater on,' Drusilla said. 'Leave the necklace, though, it's lovely.'

Drusilla cast a professional eye over the naked Yvonne as she emerged nervously from behind the screen. Overweight and plump in the wrong places, but not as bad as she'd feared. With a little cheating she'd be able to paint a flattering picture in the style of a Rubens figure. She smiled sardonically. That should please Harry Weston. She turned her attention to putting her sitter at ease.

'Your figure's just right, Yvonne. Mature and nicely rounded. I like that in a woman.'

Yvonne brightened. Straightening her shoulders, she stood boldly like an Amazon, breasts thrust forward.

'I think you'll look better reclining,' Drusilla said quickly. 'Come over to the couch and let me put you in a comfortable position.'

Obediently, Yvonne lay down on the couch and allowed Drusilla to arrange her in different poses. To her relief, Drusilla produced a length of gauzy material and began draping it in different ways over her breasts and pubic area. She must remember everything Drusilla was saying and doing, she told herself, so she could retail it to her friends later. None of them had ever had their picture painted.

Satisfied at last, Drusilla pinned a fresh sheet of cartridge paper to her drawing-board and lit a cigarette. She frowned at Yvonne for a moment then picked up a charcoal pencil and began sketching.

A short time later, she suddenly put down her pencil and said, 'Take a break, Yvonne. I need to pop up to the house for a moment.'

27

While she was away Yvonne wandered around the studio peering at sketches and paintings of landscapes and nudes. She thought she recognised one landscape and bent down to look at it closely. Her eye was caught by a drawing behind it lying on its side. Moving the landscape aside, she stood the drawing upright then saw what it was and caught her breath in shock.

The large pen and ink drawing was of Rick Layton standing naked in the studio doorway, a hand raised to the doorframe. He was rampant, his penis engorged and erect, and he was looking straight at her.

'Magnificent brute, isn't he?'

Yvonne jumped. Drusilla had returned and come up quietly behind her.

'Er-yes. Yes, I suppose he is.'

In her confusion she bent and pushed the landscape painting in front of the drawing again except that now it only covered Rick Layton up to his knees.

At the end of the session Drusilla invited Yvonne up to the house for a drink. Her brief absence earlier had been prompted by the unexpected sound of Rick's car in the drive. They'd met on the patio.

'I've come home early to have a word with Yvonne,' Rick had said. 'Ask her in for a drink when you've finished the sitting, and then leave us alone for a while.'

'Do you want her with her clothes on or off?' Drusilla's eyes had danced with amusement.

'Don't joke, Dru. I want to talk to her about the merger.'

Yvonne demurred at first. 'Oh, no thank you, Drusilla. I'm driving, so I'd better not.'

'You can't disappoint Rick. He's home and he's expecting you to look in on him before you go. He'll be hurt if you refuse,' Drusilla said firmly.

'Oh, I see. Well, just one then.'

As they entered the lounge, Rick came to his feet and smiled at her. Yvonne felt her face becoming hot as her recollection of the studio drawing superimposed itself on his dark-blue suit.

'I wanted a word with you about a business proposition, Yvonne,' Rick said as he handed her and Drusilla their drinks.

Drusilla took hers and made for the door. 'I'll just go and see what Amy's up to in the kitchen,' she said.

Yvonne sat down on the sofa and took a sip of her gin and tonic. It was just how she liked it, with two lumps of ice, and a slice of lemon perched on the rim of the glass. Harry never bothered with the trimmings, saying they made no difference to the taste. But they did.

Rick came and sat beside her. 'I don't know if Harry's told you, Yvonne, but I'm interested in forming a merger between our two companies.'

What Harry had told her was: *Rick Layton wants to get his hands on the business so he can siphon off some of the profit.* Yvonne looked down into her glass. 'Yes, Harry did mention it.'

'It would be good for both our companies. Harry's built up a sound processing base but it needs my people to develop the software and bring in more business. Harry didn't seem keen when we discussed it and I wondered what you thought of the idea?'

'Why ask me?'

'You own half the company, don't you?'

Ah, so he knew that. Yvonne smiled inwardly and took another sip of her drink. It was strong, not drowned in tonic. 'I don't know anything about the technical side, though.'

'Come on, Yvonne, you were managing a data conversion installation when Harry married you. And you'd overseen the changeover to direct input on to disk.'

She laughed. 'That was a long time ago. You seem to know a lot about me. Who told you this?'

'Harry himself.' He moved closer and laid a hand over hers, his touch sending a frisson of pleasure through her. 'I'll be frank, Yvonne. Harry's installation is like a dinosaur and it'll die if he doesn't modernise. It needs new ideas and new blood, and I thought you might help him see that. After all, it's in your interest too. Will you?'

She looked up. His eyes were caressing her, arousing responses in her body. She was aware his blatant seduction was only a means to persuade her, but all the same she enjoyed the sensations coursing thorough her. Drusilla had drawn his eyes as compelling . . . demanding. Perhaps that was how he looked when . . . Yvonne reined in her runaway thoughts.

'I'll see what I can do,' she promised. 'But I'll have to choose the right moment. He's touchy about discussing business with me.'

'Of course.' Rick gently squeezed her hand. 'It might be better if you didn't tell him we've had this talk.' He smiled warmly. 'He might think I was trying to influence him through you.'

She smiled back, a conspirator's smile. They both knew that was exactly what he was doing.

When Yvonne told her husband later she was posing in the nude, he reacted angrily. 'I didn't know it was going to be a picture of you naked. Tell her I want you with your clothes on.'

'Harry, Drusilla's an artist and you don't tell an artist what to do. Don't be such a fuddy-duddy. Besides, she only does nudes.' She didn't mention Drusilla had drawn Rick in the nude. He'd only have made some obscene comment. Harry didn't understand modern young people like Rick and Drusilla.

'Well, I don't like the thought of you prancing about there in your birthday suit.'

'I don't prance about,' Yvonne said curtly. Why did Harry have to spoil everything? 'I lie on a couch in Drusilla's studio and there's no one else around.'

When Harry climbed on top of her in bed that night Yvonne closed her eyes and thought of Rick Layton. Not Rick in a suit, handing her a drink, but as he was in the drawing . . . rampant . . . his eyes demanding her submission. Surrendering to a mounting urgency, she let imagination take over, her groans of pleasure and shuddering contractions unnoticed amid Harry's panting and thrusting.

At Harry Weston's processing centre later that night a computer's internal clock moved past midnight. Simultaneously, an illegal program instruction switched the central processor from 'sleep' to 'look at me' mode. A nanosecond later, lines of machine code that had been carried piggyback fashion by an innocent program for weeks, were copied into upper memory. There they remained, ready to be inserted into another program scheduled for operation next morning, and the computer returned to 'sleep' mode.

Five

I n the morning, Harry Weston drove to Kelvedon station and caught his usual train to Liverpool Street. From there he took the Tube to Vauxhall and walked the short distance to his office overlooking the Albert Embankment.

Six months ago he'd signed a contract with Richard Layton under which his software firm in Colchester under-took program maintenance and provided software support to his installation. A few months later he'd been taken aback when Layton suggested merging their two businesses and, for all Layton's talk of improved efficiency, and the businesses complementing each other, he was suspicious of his motives.

Arriving at his office, Harry sat down at his desk and reached for the sealed envelope lying in his in-tray. The envelope contained his monthly pay advice. Like the rest of his staff, Harry Weston's salary was processed on the payroll computer on the floor below. Harry slit open the envelope and took out the payslip, glancing casually at the figures. His eyes suddenly refocused on a line of print across the bottom of the slip in capitals: HELLO, HARRY, YOU ARSEHOLE. GUESS WHAT? Harry boggled at the message for several seconds then snatched up the phone.

Minutes later the computer manager, chief programmer and duty shift leader were assembled around Harry Weston's desk peering at his payslip.

32

'Find out how this happened and the joker who did it! And I want the answer bloody quick!' he told them angrily. They nodded and made for the door. 'And keep quiet about it,' he added. 'I don't want everyone laughing their heads off.'

Issuing orders was one thing. Finding answers was something else. A check of the printout soon confirmed the offending words had been printed by program on the on-line printer and not inserted via the computer console. But a search of the payroll programs and databases failed to discover any unauthorised words.

'Are you telling me you have no idea how this line of print got on to my payslip?' Harry asked acidly, when the group reassembled in his office later.

Bill Batten, the computer manager, looked miserable. 'We've checked everything and we can't find anything wrong, Mr Weston,' he said, using 'we' to spread the responsibility. 'There's simply no explanation for what's happened.'

'It could have been a hacker,' the chief programmer, Dave Jones, suggested nervously.

Harry Weston rounded on him. 'Hackers don't piddle about with payrolls unless it's to fiddle the accounts! I assume you've verified the audit totals?' He glared at the computer manager who nodded vigorously. Harry stroked his moustache. 'This was done for personal reasons by some clever sod who thinks he can make a fool of me,' he growled.

They stood silent, no one disagreeing. Harry Weston chewed his lip then went on, 'You see what this means, don't you? If he can do this, he can just as easily corrupt one of our client's payrolls.' Three heads nodded gloomily in agreement.

Harry dismissed them and sat at his desk with his head propped in his hands. He was worried. Worried he didn't know who had done this, and whether it was one of his staff or an outside hacker showing off. Worried about the words

'Guess what?' As he considered their implication, he began to panic.

Which was exactly what the perpetrator intended him to do.

It was in the evenings Amy felt her loneliness most. During the day she was kept busy running errands, answering the door and the telephone, preparing snacks and meals, and generally making herself useful to Drusilla. In the evening, though, once the evening meal was over and she'd filled the dishwasher and cleared up, she had nothing to do. On *Jonti*, evenings had been the time when granddad lit his pipe and they sat on deck watching the terns – 'plomping birds', she called them – dive-bombing the water and soaring up with fish in their beaks. At Hawkhills, all she had to watch in the evening was the television Drusilla had given her, and that only made her feeling of isolation worse.

There were two other staff at Hawkhills but neither of them were around in the evening: Mrs Mullins, who came every weekday to do the housework, and the gardener, Arnold, who came three times a week. Mary Mullins was quite old, her face sagging and creased like a deflated balloon. She suffered from asthma and wheezed noisily up the stairs, her lisle tights wrinkled around the ankles. She resented Amy's sudden appearance in the household and the first day they'd met she'd asked, 'Where'd you spring from then? Come from the Job Centre, do yer?'

Amy nodded. Drusilla had told her that was the explanation she'd given Mrs Mullins and warned her the woman was a gossip. 'And you've got free board and a flat,' Mrs Mullins went on in an accusing tone. 'Wouldn't have happened when I was young.'

'No, I suppose not,' Amy said. 'Who lived there before me?'

'No one. Bin empty for years. Last person was Miss Layton's grandmother, I believe.'

Arnold too was old, but he was friendly and Amy liked him. With his white hair and corduroy trousers he reminded her of her granddad. She'd come across him trimming a sumac shrub during her first week while she was wandering round the garden admiring the flowers. There had only been room for a few flower pots on *Jonti*.

'It's a lovely garden,' she said.

Arnold looked pleased. 'Glad you appreciate it, girl. It weren't always like this. Pretty neglected when I first come.'

'Have you been working here long then?'

'Five years, me dear.' He went on snipping with the secateurs.

Amy asked him the question she hadn't liked to ask Mrs Mullins. 'Have there always been bars at the windows of the annexe?'

'Well, they was there when I started,' he said. 'Why d'you want to know?'

'It just seems funny none of the other windows have bars.'

Arnold stopped trimming the sumac. 'I 'spec they was put up when Miss Drusilla's granny was living there.'

'But why?' Amy persisted.

He looked around and behind him as though someone might be listening then tapped his head significantly. 'They say she went mad and they had to keep her in for her own good. Then one day she set fire to the old barn here and they put her in a home.'

'How dreadful.'

Amy waited to hear more, but Arnold was looking guilty as though he'd already said too much to this newcomer to Hawkhills. He turned away. 'Mustn't stand here all day talking,' he said, and walked off.

It was a week since a photograph of Katrina Kovacs, taken at the time of her father's trial, had been downloaded from the

Internet and Scobie had begun his inquiries. He'd shown the photo of the sad-faced young woman with brown hair and blue eyes to local shopkeepers, and in pubs in the area, but the only response had been from a newsagent's where Katrina had occasionally bought papers and magazines. The shopkeeper remembered her because of her Australian accent and the fact she worked at Hawkhills. Neither had he made any progress in tracing the taxi driver who picked up Katrina and her companion from Hawkhills twelve years ago. The two local taxi firms had not been in existence then and Scobie had delegated the task of making inquiries further afield to a DC.

It was thanks to Scobie's girlfriend, Kathy Benson, that he unearthed the first witnesses with information about the girl. He'd met Kathy when he was working on a case of kidnapping in Tanniford where she managed her father's estate agency. He'd fallen in love with the tall, willowy girl with auburn hair but, although she felt the same way about him, she refused to marry him. She said the marriages of her friends, and most people she knew, had ended in divorce or separation and she didn't want that to happen to them. So, he'd settled for living together and given up his flat in Colchester to move in with her above the estate agent's office in Tanniford.

He was thumbing through his notebook, reading his notes, when Kathy asked him why he was so downcast. He told her about Katrina Kovacs. 'No one around Alresford seems to know a thing about her,' he said gloomily.

'You're asking in the wrong place, Norris.' Kathy had lived in Tanniford all her life. She knew the area well and, since she managed the only estate agent's, she knew most of the properties too. 'An au pair working at Hawkhills wouldn't spend her time off in a dead-and-alive place like Alresford,' she said. 'She'd come to Tanniford. Try looking on your own doorstep.'

With fresh hope Scobie walked down to the Black Boy that evening and showed Katrina's photo to the locals in the bar. He struck lucky at once. Two of them remembered her.

'She was an Aussie,' one of them said. 'Worked at some big house up in Alresford. Used to come here of an evening with Jimmy French. Very close, they were.'

The other man laughed coarsely. 'Jim boy reckoned he rang her bell a few times.'

'Where can I find this man French?' Scobie asked.

'Don't come in here much these days, not since the shipyard closed,' the first man said. 'Besides, he's married now and lives up at Tanniford Cross.'

Scobie returned to the flat for his car and drove there. As he toured the streets looking for the address he'd been given he was thankful he and Kathy lived in the old part of Tanniford near the waterfront, and not on a new estate like this. The houses, each painted a different bright colour from its neighbour, with oversized porches and windows, looked like doll's houses in Toytown.

James French's house was yellow and the window frames and Georgian-style porch were picked out in a brilliant white. French himself answered the door. He was in his late thirties, of medium height and with brown hair. Scobie showed his warrant card and produced Katrina's photograph. 'I'm making inquiries about this girl, Katrina Kovacs,' he said. 'I believe you knew her?'

French studied the photo. 'Yeah, I knew her. Long time ago, though. What's this all about?'

'Her father's lost touch with her and we're trying to find her. I'd like to ask you a few questions,' Scobie said.

'Yeah, OK, but not here, for Christ's sake!' French said, glancing over his shoulder then stepping out and pulling the door almost closed behind him. 'The wife's touchy about old girl friends. Can't I come down the nick in the morning?'

'Yes, all right,' Scobie said. 'Be at Colchester police station eleven o'clock tomorrow. And ask for Chief Inspector Millson.'

James French seemed nervous as he faced Millson across the table in the interview room next morning. Millson was not a comforting sight with his close-cropped dark hair, and long arms dangling gorilla-like over the sides of his chair.

'I didn't know this was to be formal,' French said as Scobie switched on the recording machine and dictated the date and time. 'I thought you just wanted to know about Katrina.'

'We do, Mr French,' said Millson. 'And to ask a few questions. Do you object to having your answers recorded?'

'Er-no. No, of course not.'

'Good. How did you come to meet Katrina?'

French said he'd met Katrina Kovacs when she lost her way one day walking along the riverbank from Alresford in to Tanniford. At that time there was a small shipyard at Tanniford where he worked as a riveter. He was coming off shift one evening when he noticed her wandering aimlessly around the shipyard.

'In those days the way from the riverbank in to Tanniford was through the shipyard,' he explained. 'And strangers were always confused because it wasn't marked in any way.'

He'd shown her the way through the yard and they'd started chatting. As they passed the Black Boy he'd invited her for a drink and she'd agreed. 'After that, she'd often meet me of an evening when I came off work, and we'd have a drink together.'

'In other words you picked her up,' Scobie said.

'Yeah, if you like.'

'What sort of girl was she?' Millson asked.

'She was OK. Bit quiet. Pretty lonely too, I reckon. She didn't seem to have any friends and I think she'd had bad trouble back home in Australia.'

'What about Hawkhills, where she worked? How did she get on with the people there?'

'She didn't talk much about them or her work, so I don't know. But all right, I think.'

'What was the relationship between you?'

'We were just friends. Had a few drinks together, that's all.'

Scobie leaned forward. 'Some of your old mates I spoke to in the Black Boy seemed to think differently,' he said.

'Well, they got the wrong idea then.'

'Putting it crudely, you told them you'd been giving her one,' Scobie said.

'That was just me bragging.' French was beginning to sweat. 'It wasn't true.'

'Are you telling us you didn't have sex with her?'

'That's right.'

Scobie sat back again. Millson asked, 'So, how long did you go on meeting Katrina?'

'For about a year. Then she just stopped coming and soon after that I heard she'd left the area.'

'Had she said anything about her future plans? Give any hint she might be leaving Hawkhills?'

'Nope.' French shook his head.

Millson's tone sharpened. 'A witness saw a man take Katrina away in a taxi with all her things. Was that you?'

'No, it wasn't!'

'D'you know who it was?'

'No, I damned well don't!' French said.

Millson folded his arms and sat back in his chair. 'Lived in Tanniford a long time, have you, Mr French?' he asked casually.

'Yes, all me life,' French said, frowning at Millson's change of direction.

'You see, we haven't been able to trace this taxi or its driver,' Millson went on. 'And if we found him, he'd confirm you weren't the man we're looking for and we could eliminate you from our inquiries, couldn't we?'

'Ye-es,' French said suspiciously.

'So, it's in your interest to help us find him. You having lived there all your life, must know the area and people well.'

'I hardly ever use taxis and the ones I do are in the phone book,' French said curtly, his eyes avoiding Millson's.

Millson stared at him for a while then said, 'All right, Mr French. We'll leave it there for now.'

French looked worried as Scobie leaned forward and dictated: 'Interview terminated at 11.30 hours,' and switched off the recording machine.

A package containing Katrina's letters to her father arrived by air mail later that day. Following his conviction and imprisonment, Stefan Kovacs had been shunned by relatives and friends and his only contact in the outside world had been his daughter in England. He'd kept nearly all her letters, and at home that evening Millson settled in an armchair with half a tumbler of whisky to read them.

On the other side of the room his thirteen-year-old daughter sat at a table bent over a book. His ex-wife had never forgiven Dena for deserting her and choosing to live with him, and she'd turned spiteful when he won the subsequent custody battle over her. 'She's all yours!' Jean had shouted down the phone. 'Boyfriends . . . periods . . . the Pill . . . You're welcome to it! Just don't come whining to me for help when you get problems with her.' He hadn't. He'd turned to Scobie's partner, Kathy. She and Dena had taken to each other and, so far, his troubles had been minor.

He scanned the letters, leaving a detailed study of them for later. Mostly, they were about everyday matters and what was going on in England at the time. There were many references to Hawkhills and the Layton family, and a brief mention of

James French, but nothing of significance and no startling revelations. Occasionally, Katrina had enclosed a photograph with her letter, usually of herself at a family party, or in the garden. Katrina, it seemed, had been very much part of the family.

Millson replenished his drink and mulled over the letters and photographs and what he knew about Katrina. She had stood by her father at his trial and given evidence in his defence. The three years of letters she'd written to him in prison showed her to be a friendly and affectionate daughter and in her last letter, dated shortly before she left Hawkhills, she had given no indication she might leave. On the contrary, she wrote of how much she was enjoying the warm summer and looking forward to spending days on the beach. She'd enclosed a studio portrait of herself. Millson studied it. Katrina was older and looked happier than in the one received over the Internet. This was not a girl who would have suddenly stopped writing to her father without a word of explanation, he decided. Unless she was dead.

A voice in his ear said, 'She's too young for you, Dad.' He looked up. Dena was standing beside him with a book in her hand.

'Don't be cheeky. What've you got there?'

'It's a play we're performing next term. I'm learning a speech from it. Will you hear me?'

'Yes, all right.' He put down the photograph. 'What's the play?'

'*Twelfth Night.*'

'That's the one where a brother and sister get mistaken for each other, isn't it?'

'Don't know. I've only learned this bit so I can audition for the part.'

Millson nodded. 'OK, then, let's hear it.'

41

Six

The following morning, after four days and four nights of worry, Harry Weston's fears were realised. This time it was his staff's weekly payroll that was corrupted. Seconds into the print run, after the routine check of the first few payslips, a line of rogue print started appearing on the remainder of the payslips. From then on the process was automatic. The slips were fed to an enveloping machine, stuffed into window envelopes, sealed, and deposited in the output hopper. An internal messenger then sorted them into workstations and delivered them to the staff.

When the weekly-paid staff opened the envelopes they found a line of print beneath the figures on their payslip: ARE YOU SURE YOUR PAY IS RIGHT? A worried VDU operator showed her payslip to a supervisor. The supervisor checked with the other girls and took the payslips to the computer manager.

'All of them?' he asked. She nodded and he went white. 'He'll go raving mad.'

Harry Weston was controlled and cold, however, as he listened to the computer manager and stared at the payslips. He spoke through tight lips. 'This isn't a joke any more. The bastard's out to wreck us and God knows what else he's done. We can't continue processing until this is sorted out.'

The computer manager said nervously, 'We went through all the program listings, flowcharts and documentation last time it happened, Mr Weston. I don't know of anything more we can do. The chief programmer wants to call in a software specialist – someone from Layton's outfit in Colchester.'

Harry stood up and went to the window and gazed out over the Thames, fingering his toothbrush moustache. Yesterday, his wife had brought up the question of a merger with Richard Layton.

'Who's been putting ideas into your head?' he'd asked her.

'No one,' Yvonne said. 'You mentioned it yourself the night Rick and Drusilla came to dinner.'

'Yes, but it was Layton's idea, not mine. Why this interest of yours now?'

'No particular reason. It's just that I want what's best for the business. After all, it's half mine,' she reminded him.

He said sourly, 'I see. You're going to thrust your father's loan down my throat now, are you?'

'No, Harry, I'm not. But I do have the right to a say in the matter.'

'All right, I'll think about it,' he'd promised.

The computer manager misunderstood Harry Weston's hesitation. 'If you're worried about the cost, Mr Weston, I can make it a "No cure – no pay" arrangement.'

Harry sucked his cheeks. It wasn't the cost he minded. What irked him was Rick Layton knowing about his diffi-culties. He turned back from the window. 'All right,' he muttered. 'Give them a call.'

The computer manger heaved a sigh of relief and hurried out. Harry Weston sat down at his desk again, his thoughts still on Richard Layton. Could Layton himself be behind the hacking? It seemed unlikely. Layton would want the business to continue as a profitable concern, not put him out of business. He tugged at his moustache, pulling his upper lip out of shape. He could see the advantages of merging their two concerns but he knew practically nothing about this man who was so keen to join him in business. He needed to know a lot more about Richard Layton before he agreed to a joint venture with him.

Harry reached for his copy of *Yellow Pages* for the Colchester area and selected a detective agency with impressive-sounding credentials. He supplied particulars of Richard Layton's company and his home address and asked them to make a report on his finances and business associates. 'I want to know about his private life too,' he added. 'Girl friends and so on.' The man probably had a mistress somewhere. That would cool Yvonne's interest in him, Harry thought. He was suspicious of her sudden support for Rick Layton.

Earlier that morning Millson had called Scobie in to his room and handed him the bundle of letters. 'Katrina's letters to her father, Norris. Have a read through them and get copies made of the photos.'

Scobie returned an hour later. 'Katrina seems to have been on good terms with the family but, apart from that, I can't see the letters tell us anything,' he said.

'They tell us the girl's dead, Norris,' Millson said impatiently. 'It's obvious from the tone of them she'd still be writing to her father if she were alive.'

'We've no evidence of any crime, though.'

'No, but until I have a satisfactory explanation for her disappearance I'm treating it as suspicious. We need to identify and check the men she met or had contact with, particularly the one she went away with, and the taxi driver. We'll start with the men in those photos. Fix up to see Mrs Layton. She should be able to put a name to some of them.'

'Watch out for the dogs,' Scobie warned as they approached the gate of Constance Layton's cottage in Little

Bentley. 'She keeps a wicked-looking pair of German Shepherds.'

However, there was no sign of Romulus and Remus as they walked up the path. 'I've put the dogs in their kennels at the rear,' Constance Layton said as she opened the door and saw Scobie looking behind him. The jeans and wellies she'd worn the last time he called had been replaced by a summer dress and sandals.

'A Chief Inspector?' Her eyebrows rose when Millson introduced himself. 'Isn't that rather unusual for tracing a missing girl?'

'Not if we're worried for her safety,' Millson told her, as they followed her into the small front room and took seats around a low coffee table. He took the photos from his pocket and laid them on the table. 'We need your help, Mrs Layton. Can you identify the men in these photographs for us?'

'Where did you get these?' She leaned forward to look at them.

'They're ones Katrina sent her father.'

'I see.' She bent closer to scrutinise them. 'These are family photos taken at Hawkhills. I don't see how they will help you trace Katrina.'

'If you wouldn't mind identifying just the men for us, please, Mrs Layton.'

'Very well. But I find this rather offensive,' she said curtly. She picked up a group photograph. 'This must have been taken soon after Katrina arrived.' She pointed with her finger. 'That's Clifford, my husband. He died some years ago. The other man is his brother, Lionel. Lionel and his family lived at Hawkhills then.'

Scobie took out his notebook. 'May we have his address, please, Mrs Layton?'

'Really, this is ridiculous! Lionel won't know where the wretched girl is hiding herself.'

45

Millson said sharply, 'Katrina isn't hiding herself, Mrs Layton. She's dead.'

She jumped at the tone of his voice. 'How do you know?'

'From her letters. It's clear she was fond of her father. She wouldn't have stopped writing unless something had happened to her.'

'Oh.' She sat back in her chair. After a pause she dictated the address to Scobie. She put the photo down and picked up another. 'This was a Christmas party. There's Clifford and Lionel again. The other man is the father of the little girl there who was Drusilla's friend. I don't recall their name, but Drusilla might remember.' She glanced at the remaining photos. 'That seems to account for the men.'

Scobie pointed to a photo. 'What about that one in the garden with his arms round Katrina and Drusilla?'

'He's hardly a man, Sergeant. That's Drusilla's cousin, Rick, and he was only about fifteen then.' She added waspishly, 'And you know where he lives.' She turned to Millson. 'Is that all, Chief Inspector?'

'Not quite,' Millson said. 'Tell us about Katrina, Mrs Layton. What was she like?'

'A bit sad and rather plain, I thought. But she got on well with the family and she was a good worker. There were six in the household then and it was hard work.'

'Did you know she was meeting a man called James French?'

She arched her eyebrows. 'No, I didn't. As I told your sergeant, Katrina was secretive. She told us hardly anything about herself and she certainly never confided in me.'

Scobie asked, 'Might she have confided in someone else, Mrs Layton? Your brother-in-law or his wife, perhaps?'

'It's possible, I suppose. Although they'd moved out by the time she left Hawkhills.'

Millson stood up. 'Well, thank you for your help, Mrs Layton, that's all we need to bother you with for now.'

She nodded and came to her feet. At the door she asked casually, 'This man French. Could he be the man she went off with?'

'It's a possibility,' Millson said. 'We're looking into it.'

Earl Grey arrived at Harry Weston's installation within two hours of the call. He'd been nicknamed 'Earl' because he was addicted to Earl Grey tea and carried a supply of it about with him. Grey was in his early thirties, with dark hair prematurely streaked with white, and had a deceptively causal air about him.

He listened carefully as the chief programmer, Dave Jones, elaborated the outline he'd given over the phone. 'There are no outside lines and no terminal access. It's a totally closed system,' Jones ended.

'Uh-huh.' Grey studied the flowcharts laid out for him on a table. 'Talk me through it.'

Halfway through the explanation Grey interrupted. 'What's happening here?' He pointed to a symbol on the chart.

'Just a sort routine,' Jones told him. 'The payroll's in national insurance number order and we sort it to alphabetic before printing.'

'Have you checked it?'

'No. It's a standard sub-routine supplied by the manufacturer. We've always used it. Besides, it's encrypted and it's impossible to break into the manufacturer's software.'

Grey said mildly, 'Nothing's impossible when it comes to hacking, my friend. I suggest you check the routine against the manufacturer's original version.'

Jones shrugged. 'OK, but it's a waste of time.' He sat down at a terminal and pecked at the keys. He peered at the screen. 'That's odd,' he said. 'The disk copy is nearly 2K longer than the manufacturer's copy. That shouldn't be.'

Grey nodded. 'So, let's see what's in there as shouldn't be.'

Jones pursed his lips. 'I don't know how to do that,' he said.

'Read the program into upper memory, convert it to machine code and print it out.' Grey told him.

'It'll be in machine code and hexadecimal.'

'That's right,' said Grey.

Jones stared at him. 'You read machine code?'

'Of course.'

'Strewth!' Jones turned back to his terminal.

Some minutes later, with the printout laid out on the table, Grey began working through the closely printed lines of figures.

Half an hour later he ringed a block with a pencil and straightened up. 'Illegal coding,' he said. 'With a timing loop to delay operation until a specified date and program. It's set to operate again in five days from now.'

Jones was aghast. 'That's when we run the four-weekly payroll for one of the City banks. We'll be ruined if that goes wrong.'

'Don't worry. It's easy enough to fix. Just delete the corrupted program and reload the clean version.'

'But how did someone get into the system? The current password is only known to me and Mr Weston and we change it every week.'

Grey smiled slyly. 'Some programmers leave themselves a way in of their own. It's called backdoor entry and saves time when they're debugging. They're supposed to delete it when they've finished but the geeks often leave it so they can have a key of their own no one knows about. Gives them a feeling of power.'

'So, how can we find out who it was? There were over a dozen programmers employed here when we were setting up this suite of programs.'

'Well, this guy was good. Exceptionally good. This is a

brilliant piece of malicious coding. The next time through the loop it would have overwritten itself leaving no trace it ever existed. Who did you have capable of work like that?'

Dave Jones frowned and shook his head.

'Someone with a grudge against your boss perhaps,' Grey suggested. He saw Jones suddenly blink. 'Weston will ask you,' he warned.

'I can't think of anyone,' Jones lied.

Harry Weston listened impassively while Grey and Jones explained what had been done and how the system had been infiltrated. As the consequences dawned on him and he grasped the ingenuity of the time delay and self-destruct device, his face darkened with anger.

'Total disaster,' he muttered. 'It would have been total disaster. The bank would have sued for compensation. We'd have lost every client and I'd have been ruined . . . bankrupted.' His mouth began to quiver with fury. He glared at Jones. 'Who did this to me?'

'I don't know,' Dave Jones said. 'No one working here now. It would have been planted some time ago.'

'Very well, get me the names of the programmers who've left in the last year,' Harry Weston growled. 'And their aptitude-test marks. This guy would have been pretty bright, wouldn't he?'

'A genius.' Dave Jones could have bitten his tongue off.

Weston pounced. 'That means you've got a good idea who it was!'

'It's only a possibility, Mr Weston. And there's no way we could prove it,' Jones said anxiously.

'Prove? Prove? I don't give a shit about proving anything!' Weston snarled. 'What's his name?' Jones hesitated. 'His name!' Weston howled.

Jones swallowed. 'Brian Hall,' he said.

'Hall?' Harry Weston frowned in thought. 'Hall,' he repeated in a different tone. 'I remember him.' His eyes gleamed balefully. 'Where is he now?'

'I don't know . . . really I don't,' Jones said, expecting Weston to fly into a temper again.

Harry Weston just nodded, though. 'All right, bring me his file.' He turned. 'That's all. Thank you, Grey,' he said abruptly and dismissed them both with a wave of his hand.

Outside in the corridor Jones said with relief, 'Phew! He took it better than I expected in the end.'

'Don't be so sure.' Grey's face was sombre. 'There were tears in the corners of his eyes. Inside, he's raging.'

After Jones had brought him Brian Hall's file Harry Weston sat at his desk reading it. He remembered Brian Hall well. Clever, cocky and small. Oh, yes, he remembered little Brian. And why he'd sacked him. This was Brian's revenge. A malicious plan to destroy his business and bring him to his knees. Harry's hands clenched in anguish, nails digging into his palms, as he contemplated his near downfall. 'I'll have you hung up by your bollocks for this, you little sod!' he mouthed.

Opening a desk drawer he took out a notebook and looked up a telephone number. It was an unlisted agency he'd once used to trace a man who owed him money, and frighten him into paying. He phoned the number and gave them Brian Hall's details and his last address.

'I want him found,' he told them. 'And then I want him hurt.'

Seven

B rian Hall was short, barely five foot two, with dark wavy hair and big brown eyes. He was twenty-four and he lived in a neat little house with a neat little wife, Elaine, who was no taller than him even in her high heels. Brian led a clean, orderly life. He'd been brought up by his grandmother and Cleanliness and Order were Gods he'd been taught to worship in childhood.

'Cleanliness is next to Godliness,' his grandma would proclaim as she scrubbed little Brian in the bath. Her regime had begun with potty-training and Brian learned to control his bodily functions at an early age.

Brian learned to observe her other maxim, 'A place for everything and everything in its place,' like an eleventh commandment. Each of his toys had its appointed place in a cupboard and if he failed to put them away correctly his grandmother hauled him over her lap, yanked down his trousers and delivered a spanking. This would be accompanied by the chant of: 'Everything' – slap! – 'in' – slap! – 'its' – slap! – 'right' – slap! – 'place' – slap! At bedtime he was made to arrange his clothes tidily on a chair and, in the morning, fold his pyjamas neatly and place them beneath his pillow.

The consequence of this draconian upbringing was that Brian Hall reached adulthood with an obsessive regard for order and detail. Little wonder, therefore, he chose a career in computing where a high degree of care and accuracy was required. Programming in particular, with its strict rules, rigid discipline and slavish attention to detail, satisfied a deep yearning in him. He took to it like a hungry baby to the bottle, imbibing greedily. Programming became the love of his life, giving him not only happiness and satisfaction, but a sense of power as well.

When he left college he took a job with Harry Weston's company and quickly impressed the chief programmer, Dave Jones, with the speed and quality of his work. Jones soon put him in charge of a project to design and program a new system for processing parking tickets for one of the London boroughs. Brian's career, and a meteoric rise to the top, seemed assured. One day six months later, though, Brian's warped psyche brought disaster.

At a high-level meeting, he foolishly corrected Harry Weston in front of senior council officials. Anyone else would have kept quiet about a mistake by their boss. But accuracy was a tenet of Brian's faith and required him to put the mistake right. Matters were made worse when Weston argued with him and in doing so revealed his technical ignorance to everyone.

The next day Dave Jones told Brian, 'You're off the Traffic Tickets project.'

Brian was flabbergasted. 'Why?'

'Mr Weston's orders. You put him in the wrong at yesterday's meeting and made him look stupid.'

'But he *was* wrong. I proved him wrong.'

Dave Jones sighed with exasperation. 'Why didn't you just leave it?'

Brian looked surprised. 'Because it was wrong, of course. It had to be put right.'

Jones shook his head in disbelief. 'I don't think you live in the real world, Brian. Anyway, you're transferred to payrolls.'

'Payrolls? That's routine stuff. Any dogsbody can do it. Why payrolls?'

'Because that's where Mr Weston says you're to go.'

Brian was shattered. At a word from Weston his career had been cut off and he'd been made a routine coder. Wordlessly, he turned away and Jones was astonished to see his eyes filling with tears.

That evening, in his basement bedsit in Pimlico, Brian studied a large chart pinned to the wall. It was a Critical Path network, a network of lines and branches resembling a railway system, with bubbles along them like stations. Each line indicated an activity, and each bubble a future event in Brian's life: renting a flat, buying a car, getting married and so on. The bubbles contained three dates: the estimated date of the event, and the earliest and latest dates for reaching it in order to achieve the ultimate objective. Where one activity depended on another – not being able to rent a flat until his salary increased – the lines were cross-linked to show which had to be completed first.

Until now, he'd been proceeding on schedule along the line 'salary and promotion'. This fed in to the activity line 'Get married' for which he'd estimated a year. Now, his plans, and all the dates, were in jeopardy. He would have to find another job and start afresh. All because of Harry Weston.

A normal person would either have told Weston what they thought of him and left, or shrugged their shoulders and put up with it. But Brian Hall was not normal. To him, this was a tragedy. He'd been right about something and yet he'd been punished for it. That was incomprehensible to him, and it was not logical. He'd been dealt a grave injustice by this man Weston. Brian believed in 'An eye for an eye and a tooth for a tooth', as taught by his grandmother. Harry Weston had ruined his career. He would ruin Harry Weston's business.

Over the next few weeks Brian designed and wrote a program of malicious coding. It would lie dormant and undetected in Harry's system until a given date when it would

53

self-activate and begin wrecking his business. At the end, it would overwrite itself, leaving no trace. It was an elegant piece of programming and Brian wished he could have demonstrated it to someone who would understand and appreciate it. He hooked the program on to a sort routine, leaving it to sleep until the specified date, then looked round for another job.

Brian had never believed in good luck, only in good planning. Yet at that moment luck came to him in a big way. He was telephoned by a man called Steen who invited him to lunch for what he termed 'a confidential chat' about his future. Mystified, Brian accepted and two days later Steen picked him up on the Albert Embankment in a red BMW.

Howard Steen was in his thirties. He had long dark hair with a stray lock falling over his forehead and a large nose that supported a pair of heavy, black-framed spectacles.

'I'm a head-hunter. I steal everyone's best programmers,' he said as he sent the car hurtling along the Embankment and across Lambeth Bridge. He spoke in a rapid staccato as though he was in a race against time. 'I snatch them away by doubling their present salary.' He turned his head. 'Appeal to you?'

'It might,' Brian said cautiously.

Steen turned his head back again just in time to avoid a woman pushing a pram across Horseferry Road. 'Where's the damned horn button on this thing?' He fumbled beneath the steering wheel.

'Isn't this your car?' Brian asked in alarm.

'No, it's rented. Ah! Here it is.' Steen gave a triumphant blast on the twin horns that sent a middle-aged man scuttling back to the pavement.

There was no further conversation as they careered along Marsham Street, jumped the lights at Victoria Street and screeched to a halt in front of an exclusive restaurant in Tothill Street.

'You've parked on a double yellow line,' Brian told him as they got out.

'Who cares? I charge fines to expenses.' Steen strode away without bothering to lock the doors. Brian hurried after him.

'My business is body-shopping,' Steen explained over lunch. He spoke rapidly between mouthfuls. 'I take on first-class computer brains and hire them out under contract. My spies are everywhere. I hear you're good, very good.'

'Who says so?' Brian asked.

'Never reveal sources.' Steen took a gulp of wine, swilled it round his teeth like a mouthwash and swallowed. 'You seem the cautious type, though, so I'll make an exception. We had a whisper from someone called Dave. OK?'

Brian nodded, surprised. Jones had been sorry for Brian and annoyed with Weston for denying the company a talent like Brian's. He'd tipped off one of Steen's bounty hunters and received a handsome reward for his information.

Steen pushed his spectacles higher on his nose and whipped out a pen. He did some calculations on a table napkin, wrote out a figure and showed it to Brian. 'That's what I'll pay you.'

Brian's eyes widened at the amount. He could marry, buy a house and be back on schedule with his life plan. 'What's the job?' he asked.

'You'll be under contract. You take any job you're given. Is it a deal?'

Brian's brown eyes glowed. 'Yes.'

'Good.' A cheque book appeared like magic. Steen wrote out a cheque and handed it to him together with a card. 'There's my card and a month's salary. Report to my office eight o'clock tomorrow morning to sign the contract.'

The BMW was hemmed in nose to bumper by two other cars when they returned to it. Steen shunted it backwards and forwards against the other cars' bumpers to make space to get out then accelerated away.

The August sun blazed from a cloudless sky making the afternoon exceptionally hot the next time Yvonne visited Hawkhills for a sitting with Drusilla. Although the translucent blinds were drawn to across the glazed roof of the studio, it was still sweltering inside and Yvonne was glad to take off her clothes. Even then, her skin stuck to the leather couch with the heat. Drusilla was working in oils now. After a while she laid down the palette and wiped the perspiration from her forehead with the hem of her smock.

'This heat's killing. It's too hot to work. What say we have a dip in the pool, Yvonne?'

'That would be lovely except I haven't a costume.'

'You don't need one.'

Drusilla unzipped her smock and let it fall to the floor. Yvonne was startled to see she wore nothing underneath. 'Come on, I'll race you to the pool!'

'OK!' Yvonne jumped up from the couch and charged after her.

Ahead of her Drusilla's lithe figure flitted up the garden and performed a racing dive into the water. She was halfway to the other end by the time Yvonne reached the pool and jumped in. The sudden shock of cold water on her naked body was stimulating and she splashed about joyfully. It was the first time in her life Yvonne had swum naked. She felt daring and liberated as she and Drusilla splashed about, giggling and shouting.

A few minutes later, to her consternation Rick Layton came out through the French windows in red bathing trunks. 'I've come to join you,' he called.

'Not like that you don't!' Drusilla shouted. 'We're skinny-dipping. Get them off!'

He grinned broadly. Peeling off his trunks, he stepped out of them and strode to the edge of the pool. Yvonne caught her breath, seeing the picture of him in the studio made flesh as he poised, fair hair glinting in the sunlight and dived in. He swam underwater and surfaced near them at the shallow end. Drusilla turned away in a racing crawl to the far end of the pool.

Rick waded towards Yvonne, the water lapping his chest. She lowered herself so that her breasts were covered and glanced down to see how much of her was visible in the clear water. She saw her own nakedness and Rick's too, his manhood entangled in matted hair. She quickly looked up again.

'Have you spoken to Harry yet about the merger?' He moved closer.

Yvonne felt ridiculous standing naked in a swimming pool and discussing business, but she told herself this was normal behaviour for Rick and his cousin. If they weren't embarrassed then neither was she.

'Yes, but he's preoccupied with problems at work at the moment.'

'What sort of problems?'

'He said someone's hacked into the programs.'

'That's bad. I'm sorry to hear that.' Rick wondered if Harry's people had asked Earl Grey for help and made a mental note to ask him.

At that moment Amy came out on to the patio. She had towels slung over the shoulder of her light-blue summer dress and she was carrying a tray with glasses and a jug of iced orange on it. She put the tray down on a table and dropped the towels on a chair.

'Come and join us, Amy!' Drusilla called.

'Without me clothes? No thanks.' Amy shook her head.

'Let's strip her, Rick?' Drusilla began climbing the steps.

Amy darted for the kitchen door and closed it behind her.

She heard Rick's laughing voice telling her his cousin was only teasing. Amy wasn't so sure. She'd seen the gleam of devilment in Drusilla's eyes as she came up the steps.

In many ways, Amy liked Drusilla. She was very generous and not at all like an employer, although her sometimes overt, almost intimate, affection made Amy uneasy. And it embarrassed her that Drusilla often walked into her bedroom without knocking. Through the kitchen window she watched the three cavorting in the water. Rick and Drusilla swam like dolphins but the plump woman wallowed like a hippopotamus. Amy observed them much as she would have observed strange new creatures in the sea. Granddad would have considered them weird, she thought, and wished he was still around to confide in.

Yesterday, she'd visited his grave to put fresh flowers on it and stayed for a time, hoping to feel some lingering contact with him. It troubled her that he might have preferred to be cremated and have his ashes scattered on the sea. He'd never said one way or the other, but then he hadn't been expecting to die. She'd gazed at the hump in the ground – as yet there was no headstone because the earth had to settle first – seeking assurance, but there was only that special quietness of the graveyard.

On the patio, Drusilla enfolded herself in a towel, tucked it in neatly, breast high, like a Roman toga and began pouring fruit juice. Rick clambered from the water and joined her, wrapping a towel round his middle. As Yvonne waded to the steps he picked up the other towel and walked towards her holding it open for her.

Posing for Drusilla had given Yvonne confidence in her body and she climbed boldly from the water in full view of his eyes. She turned and let him wrap the towel round her shoulders. His hands slipped down to her waist. She relaxed against him, offering no resistance. He pulled her closer and she felt his erection pressing at her through the towelling.

'Be firm when you talk to Harry again,' he murmured, his lips brushing her neck. 'Remember, you have equal rights to him in the business.' He gave her a squeeze and released her.

Trembling slightly, Yvonne sat down at the table and took the glass of iced orange Drusilla handed her. 'You're very lucky having Amy,' she said to cover her fluttering emotions.

'I know. She's an *ingenue* and I adore her.'

'She lives in, doesn't she?'

'Uh-huh.' Drusilla fished a lump of ice from her glass and popped it in her mouth.

'Where did you find her?' Yvonne had difficulty finding domestic help in Kelvedon.

Drusilla stretched her long limbs in front of her and studied the painted toenails. 'Actually, she sort of found us.' She turned to her cousin. 'Amy came looking for work, didn't she, Rick?'

He smiled at her and nodded.

Driving home along the A12 that evening, Yvonne reminded herself that Rick Layton needed her agreement as well as Harry's to the merger of their businesses. What if she prevaricated? How far would he go with his flirting to persuade her? Quite a long way she thought, judging by this afternoon. Her thighs tightened in pleasure at the prospect.

Eight

Hersham's inquiry agency was located in two rooms above an empty shop in a turning off Magdalen Street in Colchester. The area was scheduled for redevelopment and at street level the buildings were adorned with bill posters and graffiti. John Hersham, a sad-looking man with bloodshot eyes, used one room for his office and the other for staff. The staff comprised an elderly secretary, two agents and a twenty-year-old trainee called Rory Grant.

Following Harry Weston's request for inquiries to be made about Richard Layton, Hersham decided to investigate Layton's computer company himself and assign Rory to probe his personal affairs. Rory was young and keen and he'd shown promise on a recent assignment. Also, he was cheap and Hersham needed to cut costs. His lease expired next year and he had to find the money to rent new premises.

'And don't go running up expenses,' he told Rory as he briefed him on Harry Weston's requirements. He lit another cigarette from the stub of the one he was smoking, inhaled deeply and blew out a cloud of smoke. 'The client obviously hopes we'll turn up some dirt,' he said. 'So you'd better find some.'

He saw Rory look up from his notebook with a doubtful expression and went on gloomily, 'When you've been in this game a bit longer, son, you'll learn that everyone is hiding something. It's just a matter of digging it out.' He drew heavily on his cigarette. 'Now, this guy Weston says there's a young living-in domestic at Hawkhills. She's best placed to snitch on what's going on there, so use your charm and get cosy with her.'

'Yes, Mr Hersham.' Rory wasn't sure he had any charm, nor how to use it if he had.

John Hersham eyed him cynically. The boy didn't realise what an asset he had in that honest-looking face. A face like that was a gift in this business. It inspired trust. People had long since stopped trusting John Hersham, which was why he hardly ever went out on personal inquiries himself.

Amy was unaware she was being followed when she walked out of Hawkhills on her way to Alresford Creek next morning. She'd once made a brief sortie to Alresford itself when she first arrived, but found it to be mostly bungalows and houses and not in the least interesting. She preferred to walk down to the creek in her time off and sit there in peace and solitude. Sometimes she thought about granddad and *Jonti*, though the memories were still painful.

Rory Grant had lost no time in starting his assignment and last night he'd driven to Alresford and slipped quietly through the garden gate at Hawkhills. After a tour of the grounds, he'd approached the house and stepped quietly across the patio to the lighted kitchen window. He peeked in and saw a young, red-haired girl putting away dishes and cutlery. This must be the young domestic he had to get into conversation with, he reasoned. The problem was, how? He returned to his lodgings in Marks Tey to make a plan.

This morning he'd driven to Alresford again and parked in sight of the house, hoping the girl would put in an appearance. It was eleven o'clock before she came out of the gate in a light-blue summer dress and walked off down the road away from him. He grabbed a map from the pocket of his car and followed her. His plan was to pretend he'd lost his way and use the map as an excuse for approaching her.

He was disconcerted when Amy turned down a lane that appeared to lead to a dead end. He continued after her, keeping well back in case she turned round because, apart from a few houses at the beginning, the lane was deserted. She walked steadily on, past a derelict church and then some gravel pits. At the bottom of a slope the lane opened out on to an expanse of land alongside a creek on the River Colne.

From the cover of a hedge at the end of the lane Rory watched Amy continue to the water's edge and turn on to a path leading along the side of the creek to the river. After a few yards she sat down on a low bank and gazed across the water.

Rory waited a moment or two then sauntered forward. Unfolding the map as he approached her, he called, 'Excuse me, but do you know where the Nature Trail goes from here?' He held out the map.

Amy looked up. 'No, I'm sorry. I don't know of any nature trail.'

He folded the map and heaved a sigh. 'I'm lost then. And I've walked miles.' Mr Hersham had said he must learn to be more forceful and not take 'no' for an answer so Rory went on, 'Mind if I sit down for a bit?' and sat down beside her without waiting for any answer.

'Seems you already have,' she said, turning her head to study him. He had red hair like her own, only darker. It was his face, though, that interested Amy most. Not the frankness John Hersham had noted, but the freckles. She wondered if they embarrassed him as much as her own did. 'I don't mind, though,' she said, smiling at him.

He returned her smile. 'I'm Rory Grant,' he said. 'Who are you?'

'Amy. Amy Foster.'

'Do you live near here?' he asked innocently.

'Not far away,' she said cautiously. 'And you?'

'I live in Marks Tey.'

'What are you doing here?'

Rory couldn't tell her the real reason. He'd always wanted to be a policeman but his background was wrong. Father unknown . . . mother abandoned him . . . in care until he was sixteen. A reporter would have been his second choice and he decided to make that his cover.

'I'm a reporter,' he said. 'I'm working on a piece about sailing facilities in the area.'

'D'you sail? Have you got a boat?' Amy asked eagerly.

Rory, who knew little about boats and even less about sailing, hurriedly backtracked. 'Er . . . no. The article is more about navigation aids and electronic equipment.'

'Oh.' She sounded disappointed.

'D'you sail, then?'

'Not now. I used to when we had *Jonti*.'

'We?'

'Granddad and me.' She turned away from him and gazed across the water, her face sad.

After a while, when she said nothing more, he asked gently, 'Did something bad happen, Amy?'

She nodded miserably. Over the weeks, she'd longed for someone to talk to about the accident and because he was a stranger, with a kind voice, the urge to unburden herself suddenly became overwhelming. She took a deep breath and, raising her head, pointed towards the mouth of the creek. 'See that green buoy out there in the river?'

Rory peered in the direction she was pointing, but he was short-sighted and saw only shimmering water. 'I think so.'

'Well, can you or can't you?' Amy asked impatiently.

Self-consciously, Rory felt in his pocket and pulled out his spectacle case. When he had the money, he promised himself, he would change to contact lenses. He put on his glasses and the horizon came into focus. 'Yes, I can see it now.'

'You should wear your glasses all the time if you can't see properly,' Amy said reprovingly. 'Well, that's Ballast Quay buoy.'

She told him of the night she and granddad had brought *Jonti* down from Mistley to Alresford Creek. Once she'd begun, the words came easily as she related their struggle to reach the Colne, her grandfather's accident, and the shock and pain of his death. When she'd finished she felt a wondrous sense of relief and a lightening of sorrow. 'That's how I came to be working for the Laytons,' Amy ended. She didn't tell him they'd caught her breaking into their house.

Rory had listened in astonishment to her story. Drusilla's influence, which included correcting Amy's speech and elocution, had had an effect and her voice had lost its stridency. Amy Foster was not at all the kind of girl he'd expected, nor the sort to be working as a humble domestic.

'Nice people are they?' He took the opportunity to ask about Richard Layton and his cousin.

'Yes, they've been very good to me,' she said. 'Drusilla paid for granddad's funeral and they've given me a nice big flat with a telly and everything.'

'What do they do for a living?'

'He's in some sort of computer business in Colchester. She draws and paints all the time. Country scenes . . . people in the nude. Her studio's full of pictures of naked men and women. She even makes *me* pose for her.'

The first time had been soon after she started there. Amy had taken morning coffee down to the studio and, as she turned to leave, Drusilla told her to take her clothes off. She'd refused and Drusilla had locked the door. 'Don't be silly. I want to draw you,' she said. 'Go behind the screen if you're

shy, and put this round you.' She tossed a length of diapha-
nous gauze at Amy.

When Amy emerged with the transparent material wrapped
around her like a sari, Drusilla caught her breath. 'You're
lovely,' she said. 'Absolutely lovely.' Taking Amy by the hand
she led her to the couch. Amy was disturbed by the possessive
and intimate way Drusilla handled her as she laid her down
and arranged her in a pose.

'Yesterday, she and a woman she's painting were prancing
around naked in the swimming pool,' she went on. 'Mr Rick
too. It's not decent people their age running around together
with no clothes on. Drusilla wanted to get me in too but I
wasn't having any.'

Rory was about to say he saw nothing wrong in people
swimming in the raw in their own garden when Amy diverted
him with, 'I think Drusilla must take after her granny. The
gardener says the granny went funny and they put her in a
home. Seems they never go to see her, though. I think that's
awful.' She turned to Rory. 'You wouldn't put your gran in a
home and never see her, would you?'

Rory hesitated. 'Um . . .'

'Well, would you?' Amy demanded.

He met her eyes and then – he wasn't sure why, unless it was
because of the reproach in them – he told this girl he'd just met
something he rarely told anyone. 'I don't know if I have a gran
because I don't know who my mum and dad are.'

Amy eyes filled with compassion. 'That's rotten,' she said,
then went on sadly, 'My mum and dad died in a fire.'

'Hell, that's terrible.' After a pause he added, 'We've both
lost our parents then.'

She nodded. 'Funny we should meet by accident like this.'

'Yes, isn't it.' He looked away, guilty at deceiving her.

Amy glanced at her watch. 'I must get back.'

Rory hid his dismay. Having 'got cosy with her', as Mr

Hersham put it, he'd been poised to ask Amy about Richard Layton's private life. 'See you again?' he asked.

'Yes, OK.'

They arranged to meet on her evening off in two days' time.

Following their interview with Constance Layton, Millson and Scobie went to see her brother-in-law, Lionel Layton. Lionel lived with his wife in a bungalow on the outskirts of Brightlingsea. He was a florid-faced man in his fifties with short blonde hair. His wife, Nancy, was thin and dark. Her mouth turned down at the corners, gaving her a mournful expression.

Millson began by asking them if they had been surprised to hear of Katrina's sudden departure from Hawkhills.

'Yes, of course we were,' Lionel Layton said. 'But why are you asking questions about her all these years later?'

'Because no one seems to have seen her or heard from her since, Mr Layton,' Millson said. 'And no one has given a reason for her to leave without a word of explanation.'

'There could have been a dozen reasons, surely?'

'Possibly. D'you have one in mind?

'No, of course I don't,' Layton said huffily. 'Besides, we weren't living at Hawkhills when she went off, so how would we know.'

'When did you leave there?'

'It must have been about a year before.'

'It was *exactly* a year, if you remember,' Nancy Layton said. 'We moved on my birthday.' There was a note of bitterness to her voice.

Millson picked up on it. 'Any particular reason for moving at that time?' he asked casually.

'Oh, it had nothing to do with my birthday.' She was looking at her husband.

He avoided her eyes and cleared his throat. 'Well, the house wasn't any longer big enough for our two families, Chief Inspector. You see, when my brother and I inherited it we were single and living at home. When we married we went on living there with our wives, and there was still plenty of space for us all even after the children came along. But later on, with Rick and Dru growing up and needing more space to themselves, and Katrina then occupying the annexe, the house was overcrowded. We decided to move to a place of our own.' He gave his wife a sideways glance. 'It just happened to take place on Nan's birthday.'

Nancy Layton's face had an expression of amused contempt. It changed to a fixed smile when she saw Millson looking at her and, changing the subject, she said, 'Katrina was a great help to us and she got on well with everyone, especially the children.

Lionel Layton added, 'And let's be honest, Nan. We thought it wise to separate Richard and Drusilla at that time. They were becoming a bit too involved with each other.'

'Oh, yes. That too,' she said. 'Not that it did much good. They still went on meeting.' There was a note of hostility in her voice as she went on, 'Boys won't listen to their mother at that age, Chief Inspector. I hoped Katrina would influence Rick, because he liked her a lot. But Drusilla had him hooked like a drug addict.'

'Give over, Nan, she was a child and so was he,' her husband said uncomfortably. 'Anyway, that's all water under the bridge and they're permanently together now.'

There was an awkward silence. Nancy Layton bowed her head and sat staring at her hands. After a while Millson said, 'We know about Katrina's boyfriend, Mrs Layton, but did she have any other friends, or meet anyone in particular, that you know of?'

She raised her head, considering the question. 'I remember

she was very friendly with Vy Rawlings, one of the domestics,' she said. 'And used to visit her house sometimes.'

Scobie asked, 'You wouldn't happen to know her address, I suppose?'

Nancy Layton shook her head. 'She lived in Alresford then, but she moved away some years ago.'

'Drusilla's mother told me your son, Richard, was staying at Hawkhills when Katrina left. He was there the whole summer, I believe.'

'Yes, he was. I told you he couldn't keep away from Drusilla. What of it?' Her voice was sharp.

'Only that he might have said something to you about Katrina's sudden leaving,' Scobie said mildly.

'If he did, I don't remember. Why don't you ask *him*? He and Drusilla knew Katrina better than anyone.'

'Oh, we will.' It was Millson who answered. 'And one last question,' he went on, addressing her husband. 'Following on what you said earlier, am I right in thinking Hawkhills now belongs to your son and niece?'

'That's right. When my brother died, his half of the property went directly to Drusilla to minimise the tax bill. And later I gifted my half share to Rick after he'd moved in with Drusilla.'

'I see. Thank you.' Millson nodded and came to his feet.

'What do you make of that little lot, Norris?' Millson asked as he carefully negotiated the blind bend by Brightlingsea Hall.

'Well, one thing's for sure. They didn't leave Hawkhills because the place was too small. I've been there – and seen inside. It could house a dozen or more in total comfort. It's more likely there was a bust-up of some kind.'

'I agree.' Millson nodded. 'What's more, his wife was needling him about it. You could see by her face she was taunting him to come out with the truth. I wonder what it was.'

'Well, Nancy Layton obviously hated Drusilla and still does. Perhaps it was something to do with her?'

'You could be right. Anyway, it's time I met this Drusilla. And her cousin. If nothing else they should be able to tell us what was going on at Hawkhills when Katrina disappeared.'

'They were only kids then, though,' Scobie reminded him.

'Children often know more about what goes on at home than you'd think,' Millson said. 'Make an appointment to see them both at the same time. I want to interview them together, so they can't confer. And see if you can trace this Vy Rawlings Nancy Layton mentioned. She's likely to have the information we need about Katrina.'

Nine

'What's this Drusilla like?' Millson asked Scobie as they approached Hawkhills next morning.

'Rude and arrogant.'

Millson grinned. 'Sounds like she upset you. What does she do for a living?'

'She's an artist. Mostly portraits and landscapes from what I saw of her studio.'

'And him?'

'He runs some kind of computer services firm.'

'Uh-huh.' Millson turned in to the driveway. 'Hullo, seems someone's looking out for us,' he said as the gates in front of them swung open.

'That'll be Amy Foster,' Scobie told him. 'She's a sort of general help.'

Drusilla and Richard Layton were waiting for them in the front room as Amy showed them in.

'You have to remember Rick and I were children then,' Drusilla reminded Millson after he'd asked several questions and begun to look irritated because their answers were simply a repetition of those given by their parents. 'And Katrina was a servant so we didn't take much notice of her, you see.'

Millson didn't see, but refrained from saying so and asked, 'How old were you when she disappeared?'

'I was fourteen and Rick was sixteen. Katrina didn't disappear, Chief Inspector. She left here in a taxi with a man and she took all her things. My grandmother saw them leave. She told the police so at the time.'

'We were on the beach with Drusilla's mother,' Richard Layton added.

Frustrated by the further repetition, Millson gave Scobie a nod to take up the questioning. Scobie put down his notebook. 'Miss Layton, you say the two of you didn't take much notice of Katrina. Yet we have a photograph of the three of you with your arms round each other. That indicates considerable familiarity with her, I would have thought.'

Drusilla eyes momentarily flashed and she glanced at her cousin. Rick Layton smiled. 'Oh, that? Well, we were all friends, for heaven's sake, even if she was a servant.'

'Do you know she had a boyfriend?' Drusilla asked.

'Yes, we do,' Scobie said.

'A serious one, I mean. A lover,' she said.

Millson asked sharply, 'How do you know they were lovers?'

'Rick and I used to see her walking along the riverbank to Tanniford to meet him. We followed her sometimes.'

'He worked in the shipyard and they went drinking in the Black Boy,' Richard Layton said.

'And afterwards he used to screw her against the wall in the shipyard,' Drusilla added.

Millson stared at her with raised eyebrows. 'You watched them?'

'Several times. Why not? It was interesting.' She returned his stare brazenly. 'It never lasted long and I don't think Katrina liked it much. Most of the time she had her face over his shoulder looking bored.'

'French lied about his relationship with Katrina,' Millson remarked as they drove away. 'Which means he could have

71

made her pregnant. That makes him a candidate for the man who took her away. We'll have him in again.'

He drove in silence for a while. Then, as they joined the dual carriageway to Colchester he asked, 'Do I look like a criminal, Norris?'

Scobie stared at him. 'Come again?'

'Do I look like a villain?' Millson asked impatiently.

The truthful answer was 'yes' but Scobie said tactfully, 'Well, not to me, George. Why?'

'Dena thinks I do. I'm due to watch her playing Olivia in the school's production of *Twelfth Night* for parents' evening and she wants me to grow my hair. I've refused point blank, and now she doesn't want me to go,' Millson said gloomily.

'When is it?'

'Two weeks time.'

'You could compromise then. Tell her you'll let it grow until parents' evening but not after. That'll add about half an inch, which is enough to make you look different. Afterwards, you return to your own style.'

Millson face brightened. 'Yes, and it wouldn't be like giving in to her.'

Scobie nodded. 'Can Kathy and I come?'

'Yes, of course. Dena would like that. And I'd be glad of the moral support.'

Brian Hall was worried. Harry Weston's system should have crashed disastrously two days ago and Harry should be wrishing in torment now. Yet there had been no mention of his problems in the City pages or the computer press. Had the wrecking bug malfunctioned? Or had it been discovered and wiped?

After leaving Weston's installation, Brian had prospered rapidly under Howard Steen, and he'd married and bought a detached house in the outer suburbs.

Brian was proud of his pretty wife. He'd selected her by computer program. First, he made a list of the attributes he wanted in a wife: she must be short, preferably shorter than himself, attractive, a non-smoker, neat . . . There were over twenty items on Brian's list. Then he wrote a program to weight the attributes according to their importance to him and went out to meet as many girls as he could.

He fed their data into his program and ran it, but after several months he'd not found a girl who attained even the minimum score he'd set for a wife. He decided to extend his field of search and apply to a marriage bureau. But then he met Elaine Ponder.

He was making for a stool that had just been vacated in a crowded sandwich bar one lunchtime when he realised a girl behind him had the same idea. Politely, he stood aside and offered her the seat.

The girl was petite and pretty. Her straight, silver-blonde hair was cut short above the ears and in a fringe at the front and the eyes that smiled their thanks at him were a greenish-blue. She deposited her plate, cup and handbag on the shelf and tried to mount the stool. After two attempts she hitched her skirt up high and managed it on the third, displaying a pair of slim, rounded thighs.

'These stools were designed for men with long legs,' she said, tugging her skirt down.

'I know. I have the same problem myself,' Brian said boldly. Normally, he was sensitive about mentioning his lack of height but he felt an immediate kinship with this pretty little pixie.

'There's room for two if you don't mind standing,' she said, moving her things along the shelf.

'Thanks.' He put down his plate and cup.

She smiled at him. 'My name's Elaine.'

'I'm Brian . . . Brian Hall.' He appraised her. Short girls,

73

he'd found, tended to be badly proportioned, with sticking-out bottoms, or breasts that made them look top-heavy. Elaine's shape was perfect. Her mouth was small and full-lipped and she was attractive, poised and neat. 'Why are you staring at me?' she asked.

'You're perfect!' He blurted the thought out loud then added quickly, 'I'm sorry, that was rude of me.'

She arched her eyebrows and laughed. 'Telling a girl she's perfect can hardly be called rude.' She looked him up and down. 'You're not so bad yourself.'

Brian blushed. Of course, she might be married already. Or engaged. Or have a boyfriend. He had to find out. That, and a lot more. 'Come for a walk in the park after we've eaten?' he asked boldly.

'I'd love to.' Her smile was warm and friendly.

Two days later he was walking on air. Elaine wasn't married, there was no boyfriend and he'd learned everything he needed to know about her. He put the data through his program and she had passed with honours. His search was over.

He planned his campaign to win Elaine Ponder with the same care and thoroughness he devoted to writing programs. He sent her flowers, said nice things to her at the right moment, and made no attempt to get her into bed.

Elaine was charmed. She was tired of men who thought only of sex. She longed for love, security and a house of her own. And she wanted marriage. Brian Hall was offering all these, and without demanding her body as a down payment. She was grateful for that because she'd been along that road before.

When they married two months later, Elaine had been every bit as pleased with Brian as he was with her.

When James French faced Millson and Scobie in the interview room that afternoon he seemed even more nervous than on his first interview. Millson weighed in to him without preamble.

'You lied to us last time you were here. You told us you and Katrina were just friends. We have a witness who saw you having sex with her regularly. Against the wall in the shipyard. That ring a bell, Mr French?'

French looked startled. He swallowed and said anxiously, 'Yeah, all right. We did. I only—'

'Why did you lie about it?'

'Because I didn't want to be involved. What would my missus think if this case makes the papers and she finds out I'd had it off with a girl who went missing?'

'All right,' Millson growled. 'But when people lie to me I wonder what else they've lied about. So, did you make Katrina pregnant? Is that why she left Hawkhills?'

'No! Look, she broke off with me the beginning of that summer and I never saw her again. It was about three months later when she left Hawkhills.'

'Doesn't mean she wasn't pregnant though, does it?' Scobie pointed out.

'Well, if she was, it wasn't by me,' French said angrily.

'Why did she ditch you?' Millson asked.

'All she said was she wouldn't be meeting me any more.' He shrugged. 'Maybe she'd found someone else. Not that I cared much. Things had gone stale between us anyway.'

Millson studied him. French seemed to be speaking the truth and at present there was nothing to connect with Katrina's leaving. 'All right,' he said. 'No need to keep you further, Mr French. But we may need to speak to you again when we've found the taxi driver.'

French nodded and came to his feet.

After the door closed Millson sighed and leaned back in his chair. 'We're not getting anywhere with this inquiry, Norris. If we don't make progress soon I'll have to try and persuade Superintendent Kitchen to approve a public appeal.'

'I'm surprised you haven't done so already,' Scobie said.

'He wouldn't allow us the resources to handle an appeal on the strength of what we have so far. Besides, I don't want the media breathing down our necks and baying for information when we've nothing to give them and there's no evidence of foul play. It's not as though we can take the usual line and say we're worried for her safety. Not after all this time.'

As Rory walked up the drive at Hawkhills to call for Amy on her evening off he noticed Drusilla's silver Porsche standing in the open garage. With hopes of owning a Porsche himself one day he stepped inside and circled it enviously.

Behind the Porsche he noticed an irregularity marring the smooth concrete of the garage floor and stepped over to examine it. It was a footprint, made when the cement was wet, in the way film stars leave their footprints in the pavement outside a cinema for posterity to gape at.

From the size and shape of the footprint a forensic scientist could have deduced whether it was male or female, and if it had been made by a child or an adult. The depth and angle of the impression would have enabled an estimate to be made of the height and weight of whoever made it, and whether they had been standing, walking, or running.

A writer, however, a writer like Nabokov, say, would have viewed the footprint differently. Nabokov would have enthused for a page or more about the nymphet whose dainty foot, clad in white ankle sock and black patent pump, had briefly rested there. Exulted about golden calves, not yet fully rounded, glistening with soft hairs below kissable knees. Speculated on lustful eyes rising further to probe the shadowy warmth beneath an apple-green gingham dress. Lingering there before dropping to the cold cement into which the fleet-footed nymphet had briefly pressed her adorable tootsie.

No Lolita had made this footprint, however, female though

it was. Nor had it been made randomly by some mischievous child finding the smoothness of the setting concrete irresistible. The imprint had been made deliberately and for a purpose.

Rory Grant looked briefly at the footprint and, being neither forensic scientist nor writer, saw only the impression of a shoe and turned away. With another glance at the Porsche he left the garage and continued to the front door of Hawkhills.

'Where would you like to go?' he asked Amy as they walked down the drive and out of the gate to his car.

'It's a lovely evening,' she said. 'Can we go to the Naze Cliffs?'

'OK.' He opened the door of his tiny ancient Fiat and was relieved Amy slipped easily inside. Some girls, especially big-boobed ones, had difficulty fitting themselves in.

'Bit small, isn't it?' she giggled as he squeezed in beside her.

'Runs well, though,' Rory said proudly, having spent an hour cleaning and polishing the car for her benefit.

At the Naze they parked by the Naze Tower and walked to the edge of the cliff. 'Isn't that a fantastic view?' she said. 'Look, you can see for miles.' She saw him peering vaguely. 'Put your glasses on,' she said.

Obediently, he took out his spectacle case and put on his glasses. He looked. 'It's just sea,' he said.

'That's not just *sea*,' she said scathingly. 'It's sandbanks, swatchways and channels. Granddad had lobster pots all over these waters and he knew them like the back of his hand. He used to take me with him sometimes.' She pointed. 'We'd come down the Stour to Harwich harbour where those cranes are, then . . .'

She guided his eyes in a panoramic sweep, pointing out the beacons and buoys that marked the channels and dangers beneath the water. She reeled off the names like a tourist

guide: 'Outer Ridge . . . Stone Banks . . . Medusa . . . Wallet
. . . Gunfleet . . .' and the smooth grey sea in front of Rory
was transformed into a network of channels and sandbanks,
with swatchways through them, and buoys, like signposts,
marking the routes.

'I could look at this view for hours,' Amy told him. 'It's like
reading a favourite story over and over again.'

'Let's sit down and look at it, then,' Rory said.

They sat on the grass in silence and below them a calm,
windless sea shimmered beneath the late evening sun. Rory
was feeling an increasing affection for Amy but his purpose,
he reminded himself, was to gather information from her and,
after a while, he asked, 'Do you live in that annexe on the side
of the house?'

She turned her head and looked at him suspiciously.
'You're very nosy,' she said. 'Yes, I do. Why d'you want
to know?'

'I told you, I'm a reporter. It's my job to be nosy,' he said
quickly. 'I wondered why there were bars on the windows.'

When Drusilla first showed her the flat Amy had not
believed her when she told her they were to keep out burglars.
Later, after Scobie had called and asked questions about
Katrina, Amy had asked Drusilla who occupied the flat
before her.

'No one, it's been empty for years,' Drusilla said.

'Did Katrina live there?'

Drusilla looked startled and stared at her. Amy lowered her
eyes to avoid the intensity of her gaze.

'Yes, she did.' Drusilla had reached out and stroked Amy's
hair. 'But she wasn't a bit like you, my pet.'

Amy grinned at Rory. 'Perhaps they kept the previous girl
locked up in there.' She saw his eyes widen. 'Don't be silly, I'm
joking. Anyway,' she went on, 'the gardener thinks the bars
could have been put up to keep Drusilla's granny inside. He's

heard she set fire to the barn and in the end they had to put her away in Ridgeway.'

'That's a mad house, isn't it?'

She nodded. After a pause she said, 'There is a mystery about the previous girl, though.'

'What like?'

'Well, about a month ago a police sergeant called and asked questions about her. Her name was Katrina and apparently she left Hawkhills a long time ago and hasn't been seen since. Drusilla told him Katrina just took all her things and left and no one knows why. Then the day before yesterday he called again with another policeman, a Chief Inspector, and they questioned both her and Rick. I don't know what they asked them though.'

Rory was in jubilant mood when he dropped Amy at the gates of Hawkhills later that evening. They'd bought fish and chips in Walton and parked in a lay-by on the way back to eat them. Afterwards, she hadn't resisted when he kissed her. Well, only a little.

Amy had remembered granddad's advice about boys: keep your mouth closed when you kiss, and don't let him put his hand inside your knickers. So, as Rory leaned over her she closed her eyes, clenched her teeth, and clamped her legs together. Instead of a thrusting tongue, she felt a tickling sensation on her cheek and opened her eyes. 'What are you doing?'

'Giving you a butterfly kiss, of course.' He demonstrated, putting his face to hers and fluttering his eyelashes against her cheek.

'Is that what you do with your girlfriend?'

'I don't have a girl at the moment. Can I kiss you properly now?'

'OK. But don't put your tongue in me mouth.'

*　　*　　*

79

Malcolm Forsythe

Earlier that day Harry Weston received the phone call he'd been waiting for. Brian Hall had been found. He lived in a neat little house with a pretty little wife. The voice on the phone asked for further instructions.

Harry Weston explained what he wanted done. But there were to be no broken limbs, no injuries that were life-threatening and no blood, he told the caller. A fee was agreed and he was assured the job would be done to his complete satisfaction.

Harry put down the phone, smiling maliciously. The long wait was over. Vengeance would be soon now.

Ten

'About time you clocked in,' John Hersham grumbled when Rory arrived at his desk next morning. 'Where you bin?'

Rory explained he'd been working all yesterday evening talking to Amy Foster and getting information and he thought it would be all right to be a little late in.

'OK, but don't make a habit of it,' Hersham said. 'So, what'd you get from her?'

'She says the police are questioning the Laytons about a girl who worked there twelve years ago and disappeared. And Richard Layton's cousin, Drusilla, has a mad grandmother called Julia Dean locked away in Ridgewell.'

Hersham was agreeably surprised. He hadn't expected Rory to come up with anything much, certainly not a police investigation. 'Anything on Layton himself?'

'Not yet.'

'When you meeting this filly again?'

'She'll phone me when she next has time off.'

'Good. Find out if Layton's got a girlfriend – or a boyfriend, come to that – and whether he's sleeping with that cousin of his. Client wants to know. Meantime, go and see what you can get out of this batty grandmother. She must know a bit of the family history.'

'That'll be difficult, Mr Hersham. Ridgewell's a secure mental home.'

'Use your initiative, lad.'

The task of trying to trace the taxi that picked up Katrina from Hawkhills twelve years ago had been allotted to a DC. Over the last three weeks he had scoured *Yellow Pages*, adverts in local papers, and phoned every number in the Alresford and Colchester area that offered a taxi service. None had any record, or remembered, a fare from Hawkhills at that time. The DC had continued the search in an ever widening circle until, about to abandon the quest as hopeless, he made a last phone call that produced a result. A Fred Parsons, who operated a taxi service from his house near Ardleigh, said he remembered the booking.

'Are you sure?' the DC asked incredulously, glancing up at his map. 'The address is seven miles away from your place.'

'That's why it stuck in my memory. I'd never heard of Hawkhills or been called to Alresford before. Nor since, for that matter.'

'Right. Chief Inspector Millson will want to see you.' The DC arranged for Fred Parsons to call in later in the day.

Fred Parsons was an elderly, alert-looking man and when Scobie showed him the portrait photo of Katrina he put on his reading glasses and scrutinised it carefully. 'Could have been her,' he said. 'You got any more?'

Scobie handed him the photos Katrina had sent her father.

'Yes, that's her,' Parsons said, studying the one of Katrina with Rick and Drusilla in the garden. 'Except she looked a bit plumper round the middle.'

'What about the man?' Millson asked. 'Take a look at the men in those photographs. Did he look like any of those?'

Parsons went carefully through the photographs again, then shook his head. 'Not that I can see.'

'Can you describe him for me?'

Parsons took off his glasses and half-closed his eyes. 'He was wearing one of them sports caps with a long, narrow peak and it come low over his eyes. Darkish hair, and I remember he had a small moustache.' His eyes opened fully again. 'Could have been any age between twenty-five and forty.'

'And it was him who hired you?'

'Yes. He booked by phone and told me where the place was.'

'Where did you take them?'

'Colchester Station.'

'I know it was a long time ago but can you recall anything they said, or what their voices were like?'

Parsons shook his head. 'As far as I remember they didn't speak at all except to pay the fare.'

Millson nodded. 'Thank you, Mr Parsons. You've been very helpful. If you think of anything more, give us a call.' He turned to Scobie as Parsons left. 'At least we now know the Layton family aren't lying and Katrina did leave Hawkhills with a man.'

'The description could fit James French,' Scobie said.

'It could fit a lot of people,' Millson said. 'Though he's certainly someone who lives locally. That's why he called a taxi from so far away. he didn't want to risk being recognised by the driver, or the taxi being traced.'

'And if Mr Parsons is right about her figure, then perhaps Katrina *was* pregnant. That would account for the sudden departure and leaving no forwarding address,' Scobie said. 'The man was taking her away for an abortion.'

'Or to kill her,' Millson said sombrely.

That night Elaine Hall sat down at her dressing-table and picked up a hairbrush. It was Saturday night. Brian would make love to her tonight. He always made love on Saturdays.

Saturdays and Wednesdays. That was the way things had been from the day after their honeymoon. Apart from when they were on holiday. And then he did it on Monday mornings as well.

Elaine's disappointment in her marriage to Brian Hall had begun soon after the wedding. She'd been so relieved and happy to marry him, so pleased at her good fortune in finding a man who seemed likely to make a good husband and give her everything she wanted, that she'd closed her eyes to everything else.

In some ways Brian was a model husband. He was never angry, he never raised his voice to her, and he was tidy. His tidiness was obsessive, though. He set out plates and cutlery in perfect symmetry, and if Elaine laid the table he would go round after her, adjusting and straightening everything. He folded his clothes at bedtime and followed a strict routine for how long he wore them: vest three days, pants two, shirts and socks one, pyjamas a week. It nearly drove her mad.

Elaine looked at herself in the mirror. Saturday night. Saturday bloody night. The predictability made her want to scream. She gazed at her reflection and paused in the act of brushing her hair to open her mouth wide and see what she would look like screaming. It was not a pretty sight. She wondered what Brian would do if, instead of opening her legs, she opened her mouth and screamed.

She could hear him in the bathroom methodically brushing his teeth: downwards on the upper, upwards on the lower. Not side to side like her. Next, he would wash his hands. Nightly rituals.

She unfastened her necklace and laid it on the dressing-table. There was the sound of the lavatory flushing. Hitching up her nightdress, she ran to the bed and jumped in, then quickly reached out and switched off the bedside light. She didn't like making love with the light on, not with Brian.

The door opened, the bedclothes lifted and he slipped into bed beside her. He murmured some endearments and then her nightdress was pulled up and a pillow pushed under her hips. Oh God, couldn't he do it differently . . . just for once?

Brian's technique never varied. Elaine likened it to sunbathing. She was laid in each position for a certain length of time. On her back . . . on her front . . . left side . . . right side . . . All the while, inside she'd be screaming. She'd go on screaming until he put her on her back again and finished.

Rory Grant was wearing his best suit for his visit to Ridgewell. It had cost him a lot of money and he normally only wore it to make a good impression when he was applying for jobs.

Ridgewell took its name from the nearby village. He had expected it to be a grim, forbidding place but it was bright and cheerful and set in pleasant surroundings. The buildings were modern two-storey blocks and the only locked ward was the one Mrs Julia Dean was in.

As well as wearing his best suit, Rory was carrying an office briefcase. The briefcase contained a notebook, cassette recorder, a tiny digital camera lent to him by Mr Hersham, and a large box of fudge. The fudge was a last minute decision. He'd bought it at his local sweetshop in the hope it would endear him to the elderly Mrs Dean. On the way here, he'd tried to think of a plausible reason for his visit, like being a distant nephew or the son of an old friend of hers who happened to be passing. None of them sounded very likely and, as it turned out, he didn't have to give one.

When he asked the receptionist at the entrance to the wards if he could see Mrs Dean she glanced at him, took in the business suit and briefcase and said: 'Bardfield and Bardfield? You know where she is, don't you? Room twenty-three, first floor.'

Rory hesitated over whether to correct her. Bardfield and

Bardfield sounded like solicitors, and solicitors did not take kindly to being impersonated. However, he'd gained admission and that was what mattered. He nodded and marched purposefully to the stairs. He'd explain the misunderstanding to Mrs Dean.

In the upstairs corridor he tapped at the door numbered 23. A woman's voice called, 'Enter!' and he was suddenly nervous. Surely they wouldn't allow her to receive visitors without supervision if she were dangerous? He squared his shoulders and opened the door.

The elderly, white-haired woman sitting in the wing armchair in a blue-and-white striped dress looked harmless enough. He glanced around. No bars on the windows and not a straitjacket in sight. The room was comfortably furnished and through a door he could see a bedroom.

'You're new,' Mrs Dean said accusingly, pointing to a chair.

Well yes, he was. He sat down and, opening the briefcase, took out the box of fudge and offered it to her. Julia Dean's face lit up immediately, her eyes locking on to it like a space probe docking with its mother-ship. As the box came within reach her hands shot out and clamped it. Dropping it on her lap, she tore at the wrapping.

'I'm not from Bardfield and Bardfield,' Rory said.

Julia Dean didn't care whether he was from Bardfield and Bardfield or Outer Space. She was busy ripping open the box and stuffing lumps of fudge in her mouth. She began chewing, her expression ecstatic and with a sigh of pleasure her eyelids fluttered and closed.

'I'm not from Bardfield and Bardfield,' he repeated.

Her eyes flicked open. 'I know you're not!' she said crossly. 'They don't bring me fudge. And they don't listen to my complaints. You will, though. You're a nice young man.'

She put the box down on the small coffee table next to her

chair and crossed the room to a bureau desk standing beneath the window. She opened a drawer and took out a red exercise book. 'I've written them all down,' she said, returning to her seat with it and flicking through the pages. Rory saw that some of them were covered with writing and ruled off neatly in places. He wondered if it was her diary. She opened the book at a page and began counting: '*One, two, three, four, five, six, seven* . . .'

Perhaps she's not so mad after all, he thought, surreptitiously reaching in his briefcase and switching on the tape recorder. Then he looked down at the page she was reading from. It was completely blank.

'. . . *all good children go to Heaven*.' Mrs Dean's eyes moved back and forth across the page as though she were reading. '*Penny on the roundabout, tuppence on the swing* . . .' She stopped and looked up at him. 'I hope you're taking all this down,' she said.

'Er – yes, yes I am.' Rory pulled out the notebook and began scribbling in it.

'. . . *thruppence for a donkey ride and God Save the King*.' She closed the book and laid it in her lap. 'That's all for today,' she said.

Rory cast his eyes around the room looking for something that might bring her back to reality. A photograph of a boy and a girl stood on the desk. He pointed. 'Are those your grandchildren, Mrs Dean?'

Her expression changed and she became alert. She turned her head to look. 'That's Drusilla and Richard. I don't know where it was taken,' she said truculently.

Rory decided to take a closer look. Dipping his hand in the briefcase, he palmed the tiny camera and stepped over to the desk. Rick and his cousin were standing either side of what looked to be an inspection pit in the floor of the garage at Hawkhills, holding shovels. The pit had been half filled in with earth and on the floor beside Drusilla was something long and bulky wrapped in refuse bags.

Keeping his back to Julia Dean, Rory pointed the camera and pressed the button then slipped the camera in his pocket and turned round.

'Do they come to visit you?' he asked, returning to his seat.

'No, oh no. They can't. They have to keep guard, you see.' She began to chant: '*They're changing guard at Buckingham Palace—*'

'What do they have to guard?' he asked, interrupting her. The interruption had distracted her, though, and she was gazing up at the ceiling. Prompted by a suspicion aroused by the photograph, he asked loudly, 'Do you remember Katrina, Mrs Dean?'

She jumped and her eyes opened wide. 'A wicked, wicked girl,' she muttered. Then, leaning towards him with a knowing look, she said, 'I killed her, you know. They say I didn't, but I did. It was my fault she died.'

Rory stiffened. 'You mean you killed Katrina, Mrs Dean?'

The question seemed a long time reaching her. When it did she looked frightened and her voice dropped to a whisper. 'She's gone,' she said. 'Gone forever.' She picked up the exercise book and held it to her chest. 'They don't know I've got this,' she said. Her voice rose. 'They won't dare lock me in that place with bars again. That's where I found it, you see.'

Suddenly, she sat bolt upright and stared at him as though seeing him for the first time. Her voice changed. 'Mustn't talk to strangers,' she said briskly. 'Speak to Bardfield and Bardfield, young man. You're not allowed to pester me with questions.'

She replaced the book in her lap and turned to the box of fudge beside her. Three pieces entered her mouth in quick succession and then she laid her head back against the headrest, sucking joyfully. Moments later – so suddenly Rory thought at first she'd been taken ill – Julia Dean's jaw sagged, her head lolled to one side and she was asleep.

While he was wondering what to do, the door behind him opened and a nurse entered. She looked at Julia Dean and then at Rory and said in a tone of annoyance, 'She's having her afternoon nap. You shouldn't be in here while she's sleeping. You must leave, please.'

'Yes, I'm sorry.' He stood up. 'Does Mrs Dean have many visitors?'

'No. Her daughter calls about twice a year. Apart from her there's only the monthly visit from you people to see if she's all right.'

Driving back to Colchester, Rory went over the interview in his mind. Mrs Julia Dean was off her trolley all right, but not completely. Some of what she said made sense. But how much of it, if any, was true?

They were waiting for Brian Hall when he arrived home that evening. The house stood on its own at the end of a cul-de-sac and as he drove along the lane that led to it Brian reflected on his good fortune. He had a good job, a nice house, and a pretty wife. Elaine was at her mother's this evening but she would be home before bedtime. It was Wednesday. He would make love to her tonight.

They grabbed him in the hall when he stepped in through the front door. Harry Weston was in the lounge as they carried the struggling Brian to a back room and shut the door. At the first piercing scream Harry gave out a long sigh. When the screams ended and there were only groans and dull thuds as the men gave their half-conscious victim a systematic beating with heavy rubber tubing, Harry turned his attention to vandalising the house.

He went through the downstairs rooms smashing ornaments, breaking pictures and emptying drawers.

Then he went up to the bedroom.

Eleven

Yvonne prepared carefully for her visit to Hawkhills that afternoon. She wore a navy-blue polka-dot dress with white collar and cuffs which she believed made her look younger, and on the way she spent an hour at a beauty salon in Colchester. Yesterday, when Rick phoned to ask if she'd yet spoken to Harry about the merger, she'd told him she thought she ought to know more about it herself first. 'After all, as you reminded me yourself, the business is half mine,' she said.

'I see.' There was a pause before he said, 'Perhaps you'd like to come and talk it over with me, Yvonne?'

'Well, I would, yes. I have a sitting with Drusilla tomorrow. Is that too soon?'

'No, tomorrow's fine.'

Yvonne smiled to herself as she put down the phone. She intended to find out just how far Rick would go with his flirting in order to secure her co-operation.

'I like your dress,' Drusilla murmured when Amy showed Yvonne into the studio. 'I'm finishing your hands and face today so there's no need to take it off.'

While she worked, Drusilla's cool blue eyes alternated between the canvas and Yvonne. From her manner, and the speed at which she was working, Yvonne suspected Drusilla knew her cousin would be home early. Her suspicion was confirmed when there was a sound of a car in the drive and Drusilla raised her eyes from the canvas and said: 'That'll be Rick. I gather the two of you want to talk business again. Would you like to go up to the house?' Drusilla returned to the canvas. 'I have more work to do on this.' Her face was expressionless.

As Yvonne crossed the patio, Rick came out through the French windows to greet her. 'You look ravishing,' he said.

'Thank you.' She brushed lightly against him as she entered the lounge.

'Gin and tonic?' He went to the cocktail cabinet.

'Yes, please.' She sat down on the sofa and crossed her legs.

'Is Harry out of his troubles at the installation now?' he asked as he handed her the drink.

'Yes, I think he must be. He seemed very cheerful when he left for work this morning.'

Last night's savage punishment of Brian Hall had brought satisfaction and relief to Harry Weston. His frustration and burning need for revenge had evaporated and he felt a new man. This morning, to Yvonne's annoyance, he'd suddenly become amorous and it had taken all her wile and tact to divert him.

Rick poured a whisky for himself and joined her on the sofa. 'Now, what's the problem with my plan for a merger?'

'I think I just need a little persuading, that's all.' She turned her head and looked him full in the face. He could take her meaning any way he liked.

His blue eyes were expressionless. 'And how do I persuade you, Yvonne?'

'You shouldn't find it difficult,' she said quietly, dropping her eyes.

He hadn't expected her to be so blatant. On the phone yesterday, he'd suspected she wasn't looking for financial justification, although he'd brought home the accountant's figures in case she wanted to see them. This outright invitation, though, was a total surprise. He took a mouthful of whisky, thinking hard about his response. He said softly, 'I don't believe you've ever seen over the house, have you, Yvonne?'

She looked up. She had and he almost certainly knew it. 'No, I haven't,' she lied, meeting his eyes boldly. 'And I'd love to.'

'Let's finish our drinks then and I'll show you.'

Moments later he stood up and held out his hand. She took it and he raised her to her feet and led her from the room. At the foot of the stairs he turned her towards him. She tilted her head up and he bent and kissed her deeply. The bargain was sealed.

Amy had been crossing the hall on her way to tidy the lounge when she saw them embracing. She stopped and waited until they went upstairs before continuing in to the lounge. As she collected the dirty glasses Drusilla walked in through the French windows.

'Where are Rick and Mrs Weston, Amy?'

'They've just gone upstairs.' Amy decided it was not her business to say more than that.

Drusilla nodded then turned on her heel and went out again.

In one of the guest bedrooms, Rick unzipped Yvonne's dress and helped her out of it. He undressed her slowly, stroking her body and running his mouth over the bare flesh as he uncovered it. She stood still for a while, quivering. Then, impatient with desire, she gripped his arm and urged him towards the bed.

In the studio, Drusilla lifted the painting of Yvonne from the easel and replaced it with a blank canvas. She picked up a brush and began painting furiously, her face intent as she stabbed at the canvas. It was an hour before she heard Yvonne's car departing and threw down her brush.

Downstairs in his study, Rick picked up the phone. A year ago, when he'd decided he wanted a base in London to expand into, his accountant had produced figures to show the advantages of merging with Harry Weston's installation and replacing the existing hardware with modern equipment occupying half the area. He could then sell off the vacant space at a considerable profit. It was on this expectation Rick had made his plan. The plan did not include keeping Harry as a partner or his wife as a mistress.

Yvonne had left starry-eyed, promising to secure Harry's agreement to the merger quickly, but Rick was not sure she would succeed. He wanted a contingency plan in case she failed. He knew about Brian Hall's bugging of Harry's installation from Earl Grey. 'A brilliant piece of work,' Grey had said. Rick decided to employ Brian to devise another and more subtle attack on Harry's system.

He rang Grey. 'That Brian Hall you told me about. He'd be a useful man to have on our staff, wouldn't he, Earl?'

'Absolutely.'

'Well, track him down for me, will you. I'd like to offer him a job.' He didn't tell Grey what the job was. Grey was loyal but he was unlikely to agree with what Rick was planning.

Yvonne believed in keeping bargains and she returned from her interlude with Rick Layton determined to obtain Harry's agreement to the merger. Rick had been a skilful and satisfying lover, raising her to heights she'd almost forgotten. She wondered if he had a current girlfriend and smiled tolerantly, not caring anyway.

'You're looking positively gorgeous,' Harry said in surprise when he came home that evening. 'What have you done to yourself?'

'It was my last sitting with Drusilla today and I thought I'd better look my best,' she explained quickly. She'd be careful not to give herself away like this next time, she told herself. That is, if there was a next time, and she rather thought there would be.

Taking advantage of Harry's mood, she tackled him about Rick's proposition as soon as he'd settled down with a drink. He was stubborn at first.

'Things are all right as they are,' he insisted. 'I don't need Rick Layton.'

'Harry, the business needs new capital and Rick is loaded.'

'Thanks to Drusilla's father, no doubt,' he said sourly.

'That's a jibe at me, I suppose?'

'No, I'm quoting Drusilla, the evening they came to dinner.' Harry mimicked Drusilla's voice: 'Daddy was in oil. He died early, poor lamb, and left me half his share of Hawkhills and wadges of money to cope with the upkeep. Thank goodness he did. The place costs a fortune.'

Yvonne said patiently, 'Drusilla was winding you up, Harry, because you were being a bore about inherited wealth as usual. Anyway, it doesn't matter where the capital comes from as long as Rick is prepared to invest it. And he is.'

'How do you know? Has he been getting at you?'

'You wouldn't listen last time I tried to talk to you about it, so I spoke to him myself,' Yvonne said firmly.

Harry's mouth twisted in an ugly shape. 'You've been discussing *my business* with Rick Layton?'

'*Our* business, Harry. I care about it.'

'Yes, all right,' he said impatiently, 'but Rick won't be content with a merger, you know. He'll want to take us over. That's what men like him are about. Take-overs . . . dog eat dog . . . no feeling for what a man's built up over the years.'

'Rick isn't like that, Harry. He's . . . well, he's nice.'

'Oh, yes? Fancy him then, do you?' Harry's tone was suddenly suspicious.

'Don't be ridiculous!' she said, a little too quickly. 'Rick is
ten years younger than me.'

'Thirteen, actually,' he said cruelly.

Yvonne bit back a retort. Trust Harry to twist the knife.
She would stay calm for Rick's sake. 'Look at it rationally,
Harry. You're always complaining about the amount of
work you do. This would spread the load and we'd have
more time to ourselves.' She went behind his chair and slid
her arms round his neck. 'That might be rather nice, don't
you think?'

Harry was thoughtful. Layton had not been behind Brian
Hall's hacking of his computer system after all – Brian had
babbled a confession as the thugs mangled him last night. And
Layton could inject much needed capital into the company.
Harry was afraid Layton would marginalise him, though, and
dominate the business. He hoped John Hersham Associates
would discover Layton had a scandalous background so that
he could refuse to do business with him. For the moment, he
had to buy time.

'Yes, OK, I agree,' he said. 'But I need to make a few checks
first to make sure Rick Layton is financially sound and all he
seems to be.'

As he looked up at her, breathing in her perfume, his
thoughts veered in another direction.

Vy Rawlings had moved twice more since leaving Alresford
and it had taken a WDC two weeks to track her to Tolleshunt
D'Arcy where she lived now. Vy insisted on being taken to
Colchester for interview 'so she could do some shopping
later', she said.

Wheezing into Millson's office like a steam engine, she
plumped her twelve stone in his visitor's chair. 'Gasping for a
cuppa tea, I am,' she said when Scobie asked if he could get
her anything. He nodded and despatched a WPC.

Violet Rawlings, née Sparrow, told Millson and Scobie she had been employed as a domestic help at Hawkhills for over twenty years. She only left because Lionel Layton and his family moved out and Constance Layton decided her services were no longer needed. Two years before that, Katrina had been taken on as an au pair to look after Rick and Drusilla, and she and Vy had become friends. The friendship had continued after Vy left Hawkhills.

'She often dropped in for a cup of tea and a chat,' Vy explained. 'I couldn't believe it when they told me she'd left Hawkhills. I was very upset. It just didn't make sense she'd go off the way they say she did without saying goodbye. And she'd at least have written to me, I know she would.'

'The last time you saw her,' Millson said. 'Did she give any hint she was leaving, or suggest anything was wrong?'

'No. She was just her usual self.'

'So, what do you think happened?' Scobie asked.

'I don't know. I just don't know.' She shook her head slowly from side to side. 'Except it must have been something terrible for her to go off like that without a word to anyone. Anyways, Mrs Layton told me she'd reported it to the police, so there weren't nothing else to be done.' She sighed.

'You must have known everyone at Hawkhills very well, Mrs Rawlings,' Millson said. 'What were things like when Katrina was there? Before you left, I mean.' He knew that if he was to solve the mystery of Katrina's disappearance he needed to understand the situation there at the time.

'Yeah, I knew 'em all. It was a nice place to work. Everyone easy-going . . . 'cept the mistress, Constance Layton. She was strict. Not with the children, though. Rick and Drusilla did what they liked. The parents didn't have no control over them, none at all. That's why they took on Katrina, see. I blame the fathers. Clifford Layton, Drusilla's father, was hardly ever there. Always going to

Kuwait and places like that. And Richard's father, Lionel, couldn't say boo to a goose. Those kids used to have parties, wild parties, I mean. With glue-sniffing – that was the latest craze then – and smoking . . . drink . . . You name it, they did it and—'

'Hang on!' Scobie, who had been busily writing interrupted her. 'When was this? How old were they?'

Vy Rawlings shrugged her shoulders. 'Eleven . . . twelve maybe.' She saw his eyebrows rise. 'Oh, you don't know what them two was like. A year or two later they started putting on shows in the barn and inviting the locals. Dress up and pretend to be Bonny and Clyde and that. I went to one of them. Anthony and Cleopatra, it was. You should have seen the things Drusilla did in the love scene. Still, they say Cleopatra herself was only fifteen.' She paused for breath. 'It all stopped when the break-up come, of course.'

'What break-up was that?' Millson asked.

'When Rick and his parents moved out. There was a terrible row between Rick's mother, Nancy, and Constance Layton. Screaming at each other, Katrina said they were. And apparently they moved out more or less overnight. It didn't stop Rick seeing Drusilla, though. Katrina told me he often came back to Hawkhills after his parents moved out.'

'He was there when Katrina left,' Millson said. 'Spent the whole summer there, we're told. Did Katrina say anything to you about that?'

Vy screwed her eyes up, remembering. 'Only that Rick had grown up a lot, become quite a man.' Her upper lip curled up in a grin, displaying an even row of false teeth. 'I think she fancied him a bit.'

'Did you know she had a boyfriend?'

'Jimmy French, you mean? Yeah, she told me 'bout him. Don't think she thought much of him.'

'Could Katrina have been pregnant, d'you think, Mrs

Rawlings? That would have been a reason to run off and hide perhaps.'

'Well, not by Jimmy French, that's for sure.'

'Someone else?'

'No . . .' She hesitated, then shook her head. 'No,' she repeated. 'I'm sure she'd have told me.'

After Vy Rawlings left, Millson reached for his jacket and turned to Scobie. 'Let's see if Nancy Layton's at home. I'd like to know more about this break-up of the family. Remember her reactions while her husband was explaining why they moved? And I wonder what she knows about the relationship between Katrina and her son.'

Scobie looked at him sceptically. 'You're surely not thinking he and Katrina . . .? At sixteen?'

'Why not? He'd certainly be up to it.'

'But Katrina was twenty-five.'

Millson's face twisted in a grin. 'Don't be naïve, Norris. What about schoolteachers and sixth formers? Occupational hazard, they tell me. And Katrina was in a similar position with young Richard.'

Nancy Layton was taken aback to find Millson and Scobie at the door when she answered it.

'I'm sorry to disturb you, Mrs Layton,' Millson said. 'But I need to ask you one or two questions. May we come in?'

'Yes, of course. Did you find Mrs Rawlings?' She led them to the front room.

'Yes, we did, thank you. That's why I'm here. She told us you had a violent quarrel with your sister-in-law when you left Hawkhills. Do you mind telling me what it was about?'

She frowned. 'Yes, I do. It was personal. And it has nothing to do with your inquiries about Katrina. She left Hawkhills a year later.'

'I'd still like to know what the quarrel was about, please?' Millson said.

The frown deepened. Then she gave a sigh. 'All right. My husband wasn't man enough to tell you, so I will. He was carrying on with Constance and I found out. That's what the row was over. It had been going on for years and, dumb idiot I am, I never suspected. Every time her husband, Clifford, was away abroad he went to bed with Constance. And me! Both of us under the same roof! It was our home,' she said furiously. 'Can you believe it? The bastard!' She was breathing hard, nostrils flaring. 'Constance destroyed my marriage and her daughter stole my son. I hate them! Hate them!' She turned aside and ferreted in her pocket for a handkerchief.

Millson said sympathetically, 'I understand how you feel, Mrs Layton.' He waited while she dabbed her eyes then went on gently, 'I don't want to add to your distress but I have to ask you this. Mrs Rawlings hinted at a romantic attachment between Katrina and your son. Do you think there was any?'

He'd expected her to be angered by the suggestion but she considered it without emotion and shook her head. 'Richard only had eyes for Drusilla. She had him completely hooked. So, I hardly think so. If anything did happen between him and Katrina it would be because Drusilla wanted it to. She's depraved. D'you know that? And mad. She'll probably end up in Ridgewell like her grandmother. I do hope so. And I hope and pray all three burn in Hell.'

'That is one very cross lady,' Scobie said as they drove away.

'I feel very sorry for her,' said Millson. 'But suppose Katrina *did* have an affair with young Rick and became pregnant. Think what a rumpus it would cause. A sixteen-year-old son and a servant girl. That's how the Laytons would view it. All of them. And they'd close ranks to protect the family. That's what they'd do. They wouldn't give a damn about Katrina.'

'You think they killed her?' Scobie was incredudous.

'It's a possibility, Norris. A possibility. Feelings run high in that family.'

Twelve

Rory had composed his report on the office PC the morning after visiting Julia Dean. In accordance with Mr Hersham's instructions it contained plenty of detail. John Hersham took into account the length of the report when calculating his bill to the client. After completing the text, Rory input the photo of Rick and Drusilla from the digital camera, added it as an appendix then printed out the report and handed it to John Hersham.

Hersham scanned it briefly. 'That'll do fine,' he said. 'I'll append my report on Layton's financial status and send it to the client. I'll tell him we're still investigating Layton's private life. Your little filly given you another date yet?'

'Yes, next Saturday,' Rory said. Amy had phoned and told him Rick and Drusilla were going to the theatre and she'd be free all evening.

Harry Weston received the report next morning. The first part informed him Hersham Associates had investigated Richard Layton's finances and were satisfied he had considerable assets and his company was solvent and not linked financially to any other company. The Companies' Register listed three directors: Richard Layton, Drusilla Layton and Mrs Constance Layton. Harry was disappointed. No excuse there for refusing to join with Rick Layton.

He turned to the second part of the report, his attention quickly caught by Rory Grant's reference to the police inquiries into the disappearance of Katrina Kovacs from Hawk-hills. Avidly, he read on to Rory's interview with Julia Dean. Rory had given a near verbatim account of her crazy recitals and reported at length on the make-believe diary and the photograph of Rick and Drusilla digging a grave in the garage. Harry flicked to the appendix and looked at the photograph. His eyes widened.

He could hardly believe his luck. He could stop Layton dead in his tracks. Armed with this photo the police would descend on Hawkhills and start digging up the garage floor. Not that Harry had any intention of sending the photo to the police. Nor of telling Yvonne about it. He was busy working out how best to use it to his own advantage.

'You can forget about offering Brian Hall a job,' Grey told Richard Layton a week later. 'He works for Steen.'

Rick frowned. Everyone in the business knew Howard Steen. Those who had suffered his depredations cursed him and called him a pirate, or worse. To others, who had turned to him in desperation when they needed help, he was a saviour, a knight in shining armour. Steen was not a man to trifle with and coaxing Brian Hall away from him would be tricky. But Brian's inside knowledge of Harry Weston's system was essential to Rick's contingency plan.

He phoned Steen and after exchanging pleasantries made his approach indirectly. 'I need another body for a while, Howard.'

'Hot body or cold body?' Steen delighted in using jargon. Hot bodies worked alongside a client's own staff whereas cold bodies worked on Steen's premises or at home. Their hire rates were very different.

'He'll work directly to me.'

'Uh-huh. A very hot body then. What's the job?'

'Sorry, that's confidential,' Rick said.

'How the hell can I assign the right man if I don't know what the job is?'

Casually, Rick said, 'You don't need to. You have a man called Brian Hall who'd be just right for me, if he's available.'

'Brian Hall?' Steen's tone became suspicious. Always ready to steal staff from others, he was on his guard against being raided himself.

'Yes, but I'd like to interview him first, of course.'

'I'm not an employment agency,' Steen snapped. 'I hire out staff under contract and you take who I send you. In the unlikely event they don't suit, I change them.'

'I know that, Howard,' Rick said soothingly, 'but I need Brian Hall – just for a while – and I'm prepared to pay over the odds for him.'

'Why him?' The suspicion in Steen's voice deepened.

'He's particularly qualified for the job I have in mind.'

There was silence at the other end of the phone. Steen's sole concern was money, and Brian Hall was a dead loss to him at the moment. The trouble with highly-strung types like Brian was they were unpredictable, Steen found. He'd gone to pieces after his house had been trashed during a burglary and had to be replaced on his assignment and sent on sick leave. Rick Layton's request was an opportunity to put Brian out to grass for a while. And since Layton had asked for him by name he wouldn't be able to complain if he fell down on the job.

'He's not available right this moment, Rick,' he said. 'Can you wait a couple of days?' That was how long he would give Brian Hall to return to work unless he wanted his salary stopped.

'OK,' Rick said.

'Good. And by the way, I've got him sewn up tight under contract. You try poaching him and my lawyers will have the skin off you both.'

103

'Understood. I only want to interview him, Howard, not kidnap him,' Rick said good humouredly.

Rick Layton's offices in Colchester were in a listed building overlooking the Castle. His room on the second floor, with its period furniture and the walls hung with paintings, contrasted sharply with the company's hi-tech premises in the Business Park on the outskirts of the city.

Brian was perched on the edge of a leather armchair. He was wearing a dark-blue business suit and highly polished black shoes and he sat stiffly upright. His body was still sore from the beating and he'd only dragged himself here because this job would provide the final piece his plan needed.

After the beating that night he'd crawled around the house surveying the carnage. When he reached the bedroom he collapsed, overcome by the sight. He would kill Weston for this, he'd sworn. And now, his plan was complete.

Rick Layton studied Brian Hall. His large brown eyes were darting around the room as though searching for refuge, putting Rick in mind of a rabbit about to run. He wondered if this small, pale-faced individual was as good as Grey said he was.

'Did Howard Steen explain you'd be working directly to me, Brian?' he asked. Brian Hall nodded. 'And you would have to work from Colchester. Would that be a problem?'

Brian's expression gave no indication this was the very reason he wanted the job. It would explain his presence in the area and provide him with an alibi when he killed Harry Weston. 'No, that's no problem,' he said. 'We're living with my wife's parents at present and we'd like to move out to a new area.' He and Elaine had fled there the same night, unable to bear the house a moment longer.

Rick nodded. 'And if I wanted you to hack into someone's system would you have any scruples about that?'

'None at all,' Brian said. Anything to get the job.

'Good. Now, if things do go that way you'll be given a room to yourself and you won't tell anyone what you're working on. Not Steen, not any of my staff, no one. Understood?'

'Understood, Mr Layton.' Brian gazed at him with the eyes of a devoted dog. Rick was his master. Rick would appreciate and reward his special talents. Above all, Rick had made it possible to execute Weston and restore his manhood. If Brian had been a dog he would have wagged his tail to show how pleased he was.

'I'll take him,' Rick told Steen on the phone next morning. 'How much?'

'I can let you have him on indefinite loan at a special rate,' Steen said, and named a figure.

Rick gave a gasp. 'That's more than I pay my top software man!'

'So use your top software man then!' Steen trumpeted. 'If you want Brian Hall, that's my price for him. Take it or leave it.'

'I'll take it.'

Steen gave a hoot of laughter. 'Knew you would, old son.'

Rory made no mention of his visit to Julia Dean when he met Amy two days later. This time they had walked down to Alresford Creek and sat on the riverbank.

'Have Rick and Drusilla gone out together this evening?' he asked her.

'Oh, yes. They always do.'

'Doesn't he have any girlfriends?'

'Not that I know of. Oh, well, there's this Yvonne . . . Mrs Weston. She's a lot older than him, so I don't think you can count her as a girlfriend. Though I did see them kissing once and going upstairs together.' Amy giggled. 'And I don't reckon they went up there to make the beds 'cos old Mrs Mullins does that. 'Sides, they were up there nearly an hour.'

This was the sort of information Mr Hersham's client wanted, Rory thought, smiling at Amy. 'Are Rick and Drusilla partners?' he asked. 'I mean, does he sleep with her?'

'How should I know? They've got separate bedrooms but I don't know if they pop into each other's beds at night, do I? Anyway, it's none of my business – nor yours either, Rory Grant.'

When Rory reported Amy's information to John Hersham next morning he was startled by his reaction. '*Yvonne Weston*? You're sure she said Weston? Not Watson or Western or something like that?'

Rory, who hadn't paid attention to Amy's enunciation of the name said no, he wasn't sure.

'Well, you'd damned well better be, my lad,' Hersham said fiercely. 'Mrs Yvonne Weston is the client's wife for Christ's sake!'

'You didn't tell me the client was called Weston, Mr Hersham,' Rory said accusingly. 'Else I'd have taken more notice.'

'No, all right, all right, it's not your fault,' Hersham said. 'But we've got to be a hundred per cent certain this really is his wife before we inform the client she's having it off with the man he's asked us to investigate. So get back to your little Amy and double-check the name. And to be on the safe side find out what this woman looks like and how old she is.'

'OK, Mr Hersham,' Rory nodded. 'I'm meeting Amy on Sunday.'

'I want to know now. Can't you phone her?'

Rory shook his head. 'She's not allowed phone calls, and for some reason she doesn't want Drusilla to know she has a boyfriend. I'll contact her somehow, though.'

*   *   *

Drusilla had finished Yvonne's portrait and now was the time to bring things to a head, Rick believed. First, he would get Yvonne to sign away her half of Harry's business. He phoned her and asked if she'd made any progress with Harry.

'Oh, yes!' she said eagerly. 'He's agreed. He just having his accountant check your financial situation.'

'No problem there,' Rick assured her. 'So, you're sure he'll proceed?'

'Absolutely certain,' she said confidently. Yvonne decided she'd had enough of Harry's prevarication. 'If necessary, I'll ask my father to speak to him. Harry hates being reminded of dad's investment but the fact is he has to do what he's told.'

'Uh-huh.' Rick's tone was neutral. She was prepared to do that, was she? He was impressed.

'Rick . . . darling.' Yvonne's voice was husky. 'Can I see you again?'

At the other end of the line, Rick Layton's smile was satanic. 'Of course, my dear. Drusilla's finished your portrait. Why don't you pop over this afternoon and collect it? We'll have a drink together.'

Before he left Colchester that afternoon Rick collected some documents from his solicitor and was waiting at Hawkhills when Yvonne arrived. He took her down the garden to the studio where the portrait, now framed, hung on the wall. Yvonne stood in front of it, head to one side, gazing at her naked likeness. Drusilla hadn't let her see the painting in progress and she'd been prepared for a disappointment. But she was delighted with it. She looked much more attractive than she'd expected, and rather voluptuous.

'It doesn't do you justice,' Rick murmured in her ear. 'You're more glamorous than that.'

She gave an embarrassed laugh. 'Where's Drusilla?'

'Out shopping. She won't be back for at least an hour.' He slipped his arms went round her. She leaned back against him, trembling with anticipation. He kissed her neck and gently pressed her towards the sofa where she'd posed naked for Drusilla. He laid her down on it full-length and knelt at her feet.

'Oh, Rick,' she whispered as he bent forward and pushed her dress up. 'I—' She broke off with a gasp, holding her breath.

Soon, the studio was echoing with her cries as she abandoned restraint.

Yvonne put her signature to the document Rick presented to her later, and it was witnessed by Drusilla and Amy. It was merely a formality, an option to buy, Rick assured her, preventing her selling her share of the business to someone else without coming to him first. She gave it no more than a casual glance in the afterglow of pleasure and his promise of further assignations. She didn't expect Rick to continue as her lover for long, but while he did she was willing to do anything he asked.

In fact, the document committed her irrevocably. It was a binding contract which distinguished between Harry Weston's processing business and his lease on the site so that Richard Layton would not be liable for creditors if the business failed and went into receivership. This would be essential if Rick had to implement his contingency plan and use Brian Hall to put Harry out of business.

Two evenings later Millson sat with Scobie and Kathy Benson in the assembly hall of his daughter's school awaiting the opening of *Twelfth Night*. Having spent many evenings reading the other character's lines as Dena rehearsed the part of Olivia, Millson knew the play inside out.

However, when Dena came on stage he didn't recognise her and thought at first one of the teachers must have taken over the part. Stage make-up, adult clothes, and some judicious padding had transformed his thirteen-year-old daughter into a woman. He peered at the woman and realised that if he hadn't known Dena was taking the part he could not have identified her.

Beside him Kathy whispered, 'Where's Dena, George? I thought she was playing Olivia.'

As he answered, 'She is. That's *her*,' three strands of memory were activated: Vy Rawling's description of Rick and Drusilla's amateur dramatics; photos of them with Katrina; and the taxi driver's 'looked fatter than her photograph'. The strands became electrical impulses and streaked through his brain to fuse in a flash of revelation.

Katrina Kovacs' departure from Hawkhills twelve years ago had been an elaborate hoax. The woman in the taxi was fourteen-year-old Drusilla, pretending to be a pregnant Katrina, and the man with the moustache who accompanied her was her cousin Richard.

Why had they done it, though? Millson asked himself. Obviously to convey the impression Katrina had left Hawkhills. And the reason for doing that had to be that she was dead. So, how did she die and where was her body? Millson decided that with no body, no evidence and no motive for anyone to kill her, he was no further forward. For the moment he would keep his revelation to himself.

Rory kept watch until he'd seen Rick, and later Drusilla, drive away from Hawkhills and then phoned Amy on his mobile. He asked her about Yvonne Weston.

'I'll explain later,' he promised. Rory was becoming increasingly ashamed of the way he was using Amy and deceiving her. As soon as the assignment ended, he promised himself, he would tell her the truth, because he wanted to go on seeing her and be open and honest with her.

Amy confirmed the spelling of Yvonne's name and described her as plumpish, with dark flowing hair, and old. Rory, determined to be accurate, asked what she meant by old.

'Around forty,' said Amy, aged sixteen. 'And she was here again yesterday, if you want to know. They went down the studio this time and she didn't half make a noise. You could hear her squawking from halfway up the garden.' Amy had been sitting in the rose garden and the unfamiliar sounds had puzzled her. Then, realising what they were, she returned to the house feeling embarrassed.

After Rory had phoned in confirming Yvonne Weston's identity and passing on Amy's information about her further visit to Hawkhills, John Hersham sat at his desk pondering. In his experience clients were seldom satisfied. If an inquiry revealed nothing interesting, they felt they'd wasted their money. And if it turned up something unpleasant, like their wife being unfaithful, they were furious and he sometimes had difficulty getting his fees paid. From the tone of Harry Weston's voice on the telephone, he suspected Harry would be in that last category.

He could bill Weston for the first report and wait until he paid before telling him the rest, or telephone the bad news to him now. A lifetime in a sordid business had left John Hersham with little regard for ethics. However, the little he had obliged him to inform his client immediately and, with a sigh, he reached for the phone.

Yvonne was humming as she returned home from shopping in Colchester, pleased with the new outfit she'd bought at Debenhams. She would wear it next time she met Rick, she decided. Perhaps she would wear it tonight too. She was looking forward to her evening at the theatre with her friend Janet Brown.

She was astonished to see Harry's car standing in the drive. He hardly ever came home this early and she'd hoped to be gone by the time he came home. He pounced on her as she came through the front door.

'You bitch! You adulterous bitch!' he snarled, spittle flying from his mouth in rage.

'What on earth are you talking about, Harry?' She tried to sound calm but inside she was quaking.

'Having your picture painted?' he sneered. 'The perfect excuse to pop over there for a good screw, wasn't it?' He followed her as she retreated to the kitchen.

'Don't be silly, Harry, I was sitting for Drusilla. And the painting is for you . . . look, you haven't seen it yet.' She went to the kitchen cupboard where she'd hidden it and tore off the wrapping. She propped the picture on the worktop. 'Isn't it lovely? I think it makes me look quite good,' she said, hoping to divert him.

'You look just like the tart you are,' he said savagely. 'That how he had you?'

'Don't be crude, Harry. What ever makes you think I've had an affair with Rick?'

'Don't deny it. I've got evidence.'

Her heart missed a beat. Surely not? Then she thought, What does it matter? and realised she didn't care any more. Harry was a slob and a bully, and she'd be well rid of him. Rick had awakened the woman in her and made her realise what she was missing. Without Harry she could start living again. The thought brought a wonderful feeling of relief.

'All right, Harry. It's obvious we don't care for each other any more so let's be sensible about it and get a divorce,' she said. 'We'd both be much happier.'

For a moment he was taken by surprise. Then he said viciously, 'You're not getting away with it that easy. You're going to own up to what you've done first. *Then* we'll talk about the future perhaps.' He moved forward.

She stepped away. 'Harry, I'll go to a hotel for the night,' she said urgently.

'You're not leaving here until I've finished with you! Think I'll let you make a fool of me like this?' He snatched a knife from the kitchen rack and turned to the picture.

'*NO!* Harry, no! *Please*,' she begged. 'Oh, no,' she wailed, sinking to her knees in anguish as he stabbed at the canvas. With the picture ruined, he threw the knife on the draining board and turned to her. 'Now I'm going to teach you not to fuck around with someone else, you horny bitch!'

She scrambled to her feet and made for the door, but he was there before her, cutting off her escape.

'Keep away from me!' She backed away from him and ran to the sink. She picked up the knife. 'Keep away!' she screamed as he came towards her.

He gave a scornful laugh, his hands reaching for her.

Thirteen

Harry Weston's body was found early next morning by the daily cleaning woman. It was lying on the kitchen floor in a pool of blood. Harry had been stabbed several times in the abdomen and taken some time to die.

Scobie was already at the scene when Millson arrived, and the pathologist, Duval, had completed his preliminary examination. A scenes of crime team was at work taking photographs and scouring the house.

'Name's Henry Weston,' Scobie informed Millson. 'Their cleaner found the body when she arrived for work this morning. She doesn't know where the wife is and says her car's not here. According to the neighbours Mr Weston has a computer business in London and Mrs Weston would normally be at home now. They haven't seen her today and no one heard anything unusual last night.'

Millson grunted and turned to Duval. 'Multiple stab wounds and he's been dead more than twelve hours,' said Duval. 'Can't see any signs of a struggle or a fight, but I'll tell you more when I've had him on the slab.'

'Weapon?'

'Well, it's not sticking in him,' Duval said sourly. 'So, unless your people find it lying around, you'll have to wait until the PM for my opinion. Can they take him away now?'

Millson nodded. Duval signalled to the men waiting in the hall with a stretcher and black plastic bag, and walked out.

'It looks as though there's been a break-in,' Scobie said. 'Scenes of crime lads are working on it now.'

'First thing is to find the wife and make sure she's not a victim too,' Millson said. 'See if you can find an address book anywhere and start ringing round.'

By mid-morning an Incident Room had been set up at Colchester police station and a brief statement issued to the media with an appeal for information. At the murder scene the search of the house continued, and in nearby streets officers began questioning householders.

At midday Yvonne Weston walked into Colchester police station accompanied by a WPC. She had returned to her house but been refused admission by the PC on duty. A sympathetic WPC had broken the news of her husband's murder to her and then escorted her to Colchester.

In Millson's office he and Scobie expressed their regrets at her husband's death. Millson asked if she felt able to answer questions yet.

'Yes, I think so,' she said. 'But this has been a terrible shock. Harry was alive and well when I left the house yesterday and now—' She broke off. 'What makes it so awful, is that we'd quarrelled just before I left,' she went on, 'and—' Again she stopped. 'Well, I feel dreadful we parted like that.'

'So, where did you go?' Millson asked her.

'To a hotel. I spent the night at the George in the High Street here. You see, we hadn't been getting on for some time. The row yesterday evening just brought things to a head. In the end I told him I wanted a divorce and walked out. This morning I went back to get some of my things because I'd decided to go and stay with my parents for a while.'

'What was the row about?'

'It started with an argument over a portrait. Drusilla had painted me in the nude and –' She saw Millson glance at Scobie. 'You know Drusilla Layton?'

114

'We've met her,' said Millson.

'Oh.' She looked surprised. 'Well, Harry thought the paint-ing was obscene. He called me names. That's when I realised I couldn't go on. It was a *lovely* picture. Drusilla had made me look wonderful. It was—' She broke off, looking upset. 'That finished me. I suddenly couldn't stand him any longer and decided to leave him.'

'So, when you left the house you were leaving your husband for good? Not just for a time, I mean?'

'That's right.'

Scobie looked up from his notebook. He'd wandered round the house while he was waiting for Millson and had not seen a nude painting anywhere. 'And where is the painting now, Mrs Weston?'

She seemed startled by the question. 'Er . . . I-um took it away with me.'

'What time did you leave the house?' Millson asked.

'Well, I got home about six o'clock. Harry was already home, and I think we argued for about half an hour. So I suppose it would have been six thirty when I left.'

'How did your husband react when you told him you were leaving him?'

Her eyes flickered. *You're not leaving here until I've finished with you.* 'I don't think he minded that much,' she said. 'As I said, we hadn't been getting on for a long time. A divorce was the best thing for both of us.'

'And for the record, Mrs Weston, what time did you book in to the George?'

'I don't know exactly. Quite a while later, I think. Half-past eight to nine, maybe. You see, it's still the holiday season, and it wasn't easy to find a hotel with a vacancy at short notice.'

'So you left the house in a hurry, not even stopping to phone around for a hotel first?'

'No . . . well, yes, I was in a hurry. I'd planned to go to the theatre with my friend, Janet. We'd booked seats for the show at the Mercury and I still had hopes of making it, and perhaps staying the night with her afterwards. But then, after leaving the house, I realised how much the quarrel with Harry had upset me, and I wanted to be alone for a while. So, I phoned Janet and explained what had happened, then looked for a hotel.' She was watching Scobie making notes. 'D'you think Harry was killed by a burglar?' she asked. 'They said there'd been a burglary.'

Millson hesitated. The scenes of crime team had reservations about the burglary and were not sure it was genuine. 'We're not sure at the moment, Mrs Weston. Did your husband have any enemies, anyone with a grudge against him?'

'Not that I know of, no. Um . . . how was he killed, Chief Inspector?'

Millson exchanged glances with Scobie. It was normally one of the first things a wife or relative asked. Watching her face, he said, 'He was stabbed . . . several times.'

'Oh, how dreadful. Poor Harry. I didn't like him, but that's awful.'

'There's a question I have to ask you in the circumstances, Mrs Weston. Was your husband having an affair with anyone?'

She looked surprised. 'You surely don't think *I* killed him because he was having an affair, do you?'

'I was thinking more of a jealous husband, or someone's boyfriend, Mrs Weston.'

'Oh, I see.' She appeared to consider the question. 'No, I shouldn't think so. Harry wasn't clever enough to keep something like that from me. I'm sure I'd have known.'

Millson nodded. 'Well, thank you for coming in, Mrs Weston. We won't keep you any longer but we'll need to ask some more questions later. Do you have someone you can stay with for the moment?'

'Can't I go back to the house?'

'Not just yet. The crime scene has to be preserved and the forensic team are still working there. Tomorrow, perhaps.'

She nodded. 'I'll stay another night at the George then.'

Scobie escorted her down to the front door. When he returned he told Millson, 'My money's on the wife.'

Millson frowned. 'Gambling, Norris, or d'you have good reasons?'

'Bit of both. I don't believe she's telling us the truth, and she's too calm about everything. Specifically, I don't buy her story about leaving the house at six thirty and booking in to the George between eight thirty and nine.'

'Me neither,' said Millson. 'What about motive, though?' He leaned back and put his hands behind his head. 'The usual reasons a wife kills her husband are: for money, over another woman, to join her lover, or under extreme provocation in fear of her life. Well, there isn't another woman, and she probably wouldn't care if there was, and there's no suggestion he knocked her about. That leaves us with money or a lover. Or both.'

'What about pure hate?'

'Ah, yes.' Millson said. 'A possibility, Norris. Definitely a possibility. I think there's a lot of passion lurking behind her calm appearance. And she certainly loved that painting, though I doubt if his reaction to it would have roused her to murder.'

At the post-mortem next morning David Duval gave his estimate of the time of death as between six and ten o'clock in the evening. 'I can't be more precise, George,' he told Millson. 'He had multiple wounds and no one blow was fatal in itself. He bled to death and could have taken anything up to an hour to die. The weapon was a sharp, single-sided knife about four inches long, probably a kitchen knife of some kind. Your lads have shown me the knives they brought away from the kitchen and none of them match the wounds. But they're not a set so it's not possible to say whether there's one missing. There were four wounds: three in the abdomen and one in the back. In the ones to the abdomen the knife went in straight with the blade level. In the case of the one in the back, the knife was held at a downward angle, like a dagger.' Duval picked up a scalpel and demonstrated. 'I can't be certain of the order,' he went on. 'It could have been three in the front, and then one in the back as he turned away; or the first in the back and the other three as he turned round. There are no defensive wounds – no cuts to his fingers or hands – so the attack was quick and he had no chance to defend himself. And it was violent – the knife was thrust in to the hilt every time.'

'Would the killer be covered in blood?'

'Probably not. The spleen, bladder and the intestines were all punctured, but there was no arterial bleeding. The blood simply oozed out, and his jacket and trousers absorbed most of it as he lay on the floor. Eventually, the heart failed and the flow stopped.' Duval removed his spectacles and carefully replaced them in their case. 'That's about it. The contents of his pockets are in a plastic bag on the table there. Nothing unusual about them.'

Scobie picked up the bag and emptied out the contents. Among them was a bunch of keys and a wallet. He opened the wallet and examined it. 'Fifty pounds in notes and several credit cards,' he said. 'Makes it even less likely the burglary was genuine.'

'Unless the burglar was too squeamish to search the body,' Millson said.

There was a message awaiting Millson when he returned to the station. 'A John Hersham phoned, sir,' a DC told him. 'He asked for the DCI in charge of the Weston murder and refused to speak to anyone else. Said it was important.'

When Millson phoned the number a voice on the other end

announced, 'Hersham Associates.' John Hersham's only associates were petty criminals and fraudsters, but he liked to convey an impression of respectability. 'Ah, Chief Inspector,' he said earnestly, when Millson identified himself. 'I can save your guys some leg work. Harry Weston was a client of ours. I telephoned the result of the inquiry to him the day before yesterday. And he was pretty mad about it.'

'Uh-huh. Why was that?'

'He'd asked us to check the financial status of a man called Richard Layton and find out if he had a girlfriend and so on. He did . . . Harry Weston's own wife. Harry was hopping mad when I told him. Next thing I hear, Harry's been murdered.'

'Do you have evidence Mrs Weston and Richard Layton are lovers?'

'Well, my man didn't actually see them on the job, if that's what you mean, Mr Millson. But the live-in domestic was very certain about what they were doing. I'm quite sure it's true.'

'I see. Well, thank you for telling me, Mr Hersham.'

'Glad to be of help, Chief Inspector.' John Hersham's tone was unctuous. He believed in keeping on good terms with the local boys in blue. Might need a favour from them sometime. 'Would you like a copy of my agent's report, Chief Inspector?'

'Thank you. I'd appreciate that, Mr Hersham.'

After the call Millson called his murder team together and gave them the findings of the post-mortem.

'Clearly, this was a deliberate and sustained attack intended to kill,' he told them. 'We need to find the weapon, if possible. So, I want a search of the area . . . gardens, refuse bins and so on. We're looking for a kitchen-type knife with a four-inch blade, remember.' Millson paused and looked round the room. 'Now, what's the doubt about the burglary?'

A DC answered. 'We don't believe it's genuine, sir. The drawers have been turned over and some of the contents thrown on the floor but the scene just doesn't look right. Villains either go through certain drawers and cupboards quickly, because they know the most likely places for money and valuables, or they empty the lot out on the floor. The broken glass in the kitchen door, and the fact it's unbolted, is suspicious too. The whole set-up looks to be an amateurish attempt to fake a break-in.'

Millson nodded. 'Right. So, this was an attempt to make us think Mr Weston was killed by an intruder. Which means the killer was already in the house, or perhaps admitted by him. Anything from the search of the house?'

'Nothing so far, sir,' said a WDC. 'But there's a safe in the study we haven't been able to look in. We haven't found the key to it.'

'Well, we've now got the bunch of keys he was carrying and, hopefully, one of them is the key to the safe,' Millson said. 'We'll try them when we call on Mrs Weston tomorrow morning, or maybe she has a key herself. Now, on the subject of Mrs Weston, it's obvious from my interview with her yesterday that her feelings for her husband were anything but affectionate. This has just been confirmed by an inquiry agent who tells me she's in a sexual relationship with a man called Richard Layton. That doesn't make her a murderess, of course, but I'm not happy with the account she's given me of her movements the evening he was killed. For the moment, I'm keeping an open mind about her.'

That evening, Brian and Elaine Hall were at Hawkhills. Brian had been surprised when he and his wife were invited to dinner so soon after he started work with Rick's firm. So far, he'd only been given routine programming and he wondered whether this was to be just a social evening, or had some other purpose.

In fact, Richard Layton was undecided whether to keep

Brian on now Harry Weston was dead. He could use him on upgrading the software and transferring the work from London to Colchester but he was already having doubts about him. Brian was very withdrawn and it was difficult to get to know him. Rick had invited him and his wife to Hawkhills for the evening to learn more about them. 'See if you can draw Brian out, Dru,' he'd asked Drusilla. 'Probe his background for me and find out what makes him tick.'

Elaine had been nervous of meeting Brian's boss because Brian told her he had a reputation for ruthlessness. When they arrived at Hawkhills that evening, though, what registered with Elaine was Rick Layton's quick smile and the laughter in his eyes. She found it hard to believe he was ruthless as he took her hand and their eyes met. Rick was in a dinner jacket and dress shirt and the velvet bow-tie had been hand-tied. Elaine hoped Brian didn't feel awkward in his grey office suit.

Drusilla Layton kissed her on the cheek. 'What a charming dress,' she said.

'Thank you.' Elaine blushed with pleasure. The figure-hugging dress was pale yellow, and she'd had misgivings about it. Drusilla was wearing black satin evening pants with a bolero jacket. Her shoulder-length blonde hair shone like gold and Elaine thought her strikingly beautiful.

She took Elaine's hand. 'Come and have a drink, Elaine, and tell me about your work. I hear you're a graphic artist.'

Elaine was overawed when she discovered Drusilla was an artist – a *real* artist, she told her workmates in the graphics department next day. However, she was soon put at ease by Drusilla asking her about computer-produced artwork, which Elaine knew all about.

At the end of the meal, as Amy cleared the desert, Drusilla told her, 'Leave coffee for the moment, Amy. We'll have it later.' She turned to her cousin. 'Rick, why don't you show

Elaine the gardens while Brian and I finish the wine and get to know each other?'

Rick smiled and took Elaine's hand. 'Shall we?'

Outside, twilight was ending and the moon had begun to brighten in the darkening sky. As they strolled into the gloom beneath the trees at the end of the garden, Rick stopped and turned Elaine towards him. Her silver-blonde hair reflected the moonlight filtering through the leaves and playing around her mouth.

'You're very kissable,' he said, and before she realised what was happening he'd pulled her to him and kissed her full on the mouth.

Afterwards, Elaine was annoyed with herself for letting time pass instead of resisting immediately. She excused herself on the grounds she was slightly drunk and he was Brian's boss so she mustn't offend him. It had been a deep, intimate kiss. When he let her go she was breathless, and her heart was beating faster because her body had responded. She hoped he hadn't noticed.

In the dining-room Drusilla recharged the glasses and brought her chair round the table to sit next to Brian. 'Rick says you're a computer wizard. That's somewhere between a geek and a nerd, isn't it?'

He laughed. 'I've not heard that definition before.'

'I read it in a book,' she said. 'Do you enjoy your work?'

'Yes, very much.'

She moved closer, smiling at him. 'What else do you enjoy, Brian,' she asked softly.

'What did you think of them, Dru?' Rick asked later as they stood at the front door watching the car lights receding down the drive.

'They're like two little dolls. You feel you could sit and play with them.'

'How did you get on with Brian?'

'I didn't. He's tight-lipped about everything . . . himself . . . his wife . . . his work. It was like trying to open an oyster without an oyster knife. And he's sexless, no response at all.'

'Perhaps he's gay.'

She frowned. 'I don't think so. I think he has a problem, something holding him back.'

'Really?' He gave a slight laugh. 'Interesting.'

'How was Elaine?'

'Well, she liked being kissed,' he said. 'But she spent most of the time telling me about the dreadful burglary they'd had. What d'you say we take them for a trip on the boat, Dru?'

Drusilla smiled. 'Yes, let's.'

On their drive home Elaine told Brian, 'There was a hand feeling my legs all during dinner.'

'Layton's got a bloody nerve!' he said.

'It wasn't Rick,' she said. 'It was Drusilla.'

Fourteen

Yvonne Weston looked anxious when she saw Millson and Scobie were accompanied by a WPC in uniform.

'We need to look in the safe in your husband's study, Mrs Weston,' Millson told her. 'In case it contains something that has a bearing on his murder. Do you happen to have a key?'

'No, I don't.' Yvonne's expression changed from anxiety to alarm. Fearful the evidence Harry said he had about her and Rick was locked in the safe, she'd searched high and low for the key and not found it. 'It's an old safe Harry once had in his office and he had the only key,' she said.

'Well, we've brought the bunch of keys he had on him so hopefully one of them is the safe key,' Millson said.

In the study the WPC knelt in front of the safe. She peered at the lock then selected a likely looking key on the key ring and tried it. It fitted. She unlocked the safe, turned the heavy brass handle and opened the door then looked up inquiringly at Scobie. He nodded and she reached inside and began lifting out the contents. As she handed them to him Scobie laid them out on a table next to the bureau desk. The first items were a number of pornographic magazines. Yvonne Weston reached out and picked one up. She glanced at a page or two, then made a face and put it down again.

When the safe had been emptied Millson stepped forward and sorted through the items lying on the table. He assembled two passports, some jewellery and the magazines together then picked up a foolscap envelope marked 'Hersham Associates' and put it to one side. Yvonne recognised the envelope as one that came in the post about two weeks ago. Harry had said nothing at the time so she was confident it contained nothing about her affair with Rick.

The only other item was a set of Polaroid photographs secured by an elastic band. Millson removed the elastic band and glanced through them. They seemed to be pornographic pictures and he was about to put them with the magazines when he came to several that depicted scenes of vandalism. He turned to Yvonne.

'Did your husband own a Polaroid camera, Mrs Weston?'

'Yes, he did. Why?'

'Do you know if he took these pictures?' He held out two of them.

Terrified that, impossible as it seemed, they were of her and Rick she took them with shaking hands. When she saw they were photos of vandalised rooms, the floors littered with smashed ornaments, she lowered her head to hide her relief. 'I've no idea,' she said, handing them back. 'They're not anywhere Harry and I have visited.'

Millson nodded. He secured the photos with the elastic band again and placed them on top of Hersham's report. 'Make out a receipt for a report by Hersham Associates and a collection of Polaroid photographs,' he told the WPC.

She wrote in her notebook then tore out the page and handed it to him. Millson signed and gave it to Yvonne. 'These are the items we're taking away, Mrs Weston,' he said. 'And now, if you please, I'd like to ask you some questions. Shall we move to the sitting-room?'

Crossing the hall, Millson told the WPC, 'We shan't need you, Constable.' She nodded and hung back as he and Scobie followed Yvonne Weston to the sitting-room.

Yvonne was relaxed and confident as they took seats but her confidence was shattered by Millson's first question.

'What is your relationship with Richard Layton, Mrs Weston?' he asked.

'Relationship? I don't understand. Rick is Drusilla's cousin. We're friends.'

'My understanding is that you and Mr Layton are rather more than friends. Was that what the quarrel with your husband was really about?'

Yvonne thought quickly. No one could have witnessed those two occasions with Rick, and there had been nothing incriminating in the safe. She decided to brazen it out. 'Of course not. It was about the picture as I told you.' She waited for Millson to challenge her and when he said nothing she went on boldly, 'And anyway, my private life has nothing to do with my husband's murder.'

Millson sighed inwardly. Either this woman was reckless or she was trying to be clever. John Hersham had sent him Rory Grant's report on Yvonne Weston's visits to Hawkhills as promised and, like Hersham, Millson had no doubt her relationship with Layton was sexual. Perhaps she was only lying to preserve her good name. He would not confront her with the lie for the present. It was often useful to let a suspect's lies pass and confront them with the truth later.

'I'm simply trying to establish facts,' he told her. 'Tell me, have you checked if anything's missing from the house?'

'Um . . . no. No, I haven't. I suppose I should.'

'You certainly should,' he said, smiling at her. Would she be foolish enough to pretend something valuable had been taken? He doubted it. 'And I'd like you to check the kitchen in particular. Your husband was killed with some kind of kitchen knife, and we need to know if any knives are missing.'

She swallowed. 'Yes, I'll do that.'

'Thank you. Now, you told us you left the house at six

thirty and then you phoned your friend, Janet, to tell her you didn't feel like going to the theatre. What time was that?'

'Soon after I left the house. I phoned her on my mobile.'

Scobie asked, 'Your friend's name and address, please, Mrs Weston?'

'Is this really necessary?' she asked Millson.

'Yes, it is,' he said sharply. 'Your husband was killed between six o'clock and nine and we have to establish exactly where people were and what they were doing between those times.'

'I see. Well, her name's Janet Brown and she lives in East Bergholt.' She dictated the address to Scobie then turned her head in surprise as the woman police constable entered the room.

Before they arrived Millson had given the WPC an instruction. 'I want you to search the house while I'm questioning Mrs Weston, Constable.'

'What am I looking for, sir?'

'A picture,' Millson said. 'A painting of Mrs Weston in the nude. I doubt it will be hanging on the wall. It's probably in a cupboard somewhere.'

Yvonne watched the WPC bend down and murmur in Millson's ear then straighten and remain standing behind his chair. He leaned forward. 'I wonder, may we see this painting of you that caused your husband such offence, Mrs Weston?'

Startled, she said hurriedly, 'I'm afraid not. I couldn't bear to look at it after the awful things Harry had said about it so I put it in the refuse bin. And by now it'll be—'

Scobie interrupted her. 'But you told us you took it away with you when you left the house.'

'Yes, but that was before Harry was murdered. After that I—'

'Mrs Weston,' Millson said sternly. 'The painting is upstairs, hidden in a cupboard in your bedroom.'

127

Her eyes widened. 'You had no right to search my house without permission!' she said angrily.

'The house has been the scene of a murder,' Millson said harshly. 'And I will search it, examine it and take it apart, if necessary, to further my investigation. My officer says the picture has been slashed to ribbons. Do you want me to have it brought down here?'

'Oh no!' Her eyes filled with tears. 'Please, don't do that. You see, I thought Drusilla might be able to repair it. That's why I kept it.'

'All right. What made Harry do it? It was Harry, I presume?'

She nodded. 'Revenge, I suppose. Because I was leaving him.'

'He didn't try to stop you?'

'No. There was no point. He knew that would finish me, and it was all over between us.'

Harry had been determined to stop her, though. And to punish her, he'd said. She'd snatched up the knife. *You lay your hands on me and I swear I'll kill you, Harry. I mean it.* He'd sneered at her and kept coming.

Millson studied her. The tears were genuine. But tears were no testament to innocence. 'I have a problem with that scenario, Mrs Weston. If your husband was so angry with you he took up a knife and attacked your picture, I find it hard to believe he then just stood by and let you walk out on him.'

'Well, he did,' she said. 'I think he felt ashamed of what he'd done.'

'Uh-huh. Let me suggest a different scenario and that what really happened is this. You were so upset and angry at what Harry did to your picture – the picture you loved – that you lost your temper, picked up the knife and stabbed him with it.'

'*No!* No, I didn't. Harry was alive when I left.'

Millson continued relentlessly, 'And then to cover up what you'd done you turned out a few drawers and broke the kitchen window to make it look as though an intruder killed your husband.'

'No, I didn't. I didn't do any of that,' she insisted. She looked frightened.

Millson was silent for a while. He had grave suspicions about Yvonne Weston. The receptionist at the George Hotel had confirmed she booked in at a quarter to nine that evening as she said, but she'd lied about her affair with Layton, and he was sure she was lying again now. However, as yet, he had no evidence to justify further action.

'Very well, Mrs Weston, We'll leave it there for the moment.'

Back in his office, Millson went through the polaroids taken from Harry Weston's safe, passing them one by one to Scobie.

'Someone's house was given a right going over,' Scobie said when they came to the end. 'That bedroom scene is very nasty indeed. Why did Harry Weston have them?'

'Because he took them – or else had someone take them for him,' Millson said. 'Which means there's a connection between him and the vandalism in some way. I wonder whose house it is?'

'Young couple, anyway,' said Scobie.

'How d'you make that out?'

'The underwear in the bedroom scene. Like Kathy wears when she's feeling frisky.'

'Thank you for the expert opinion, Norris,' Millson said tartly. 'Perhaps you also have an opinion on why the photos were taken?'

'Blackmail? Perhaps Weston was blackmailing whoever did this and the blackmailer turned on him and killed him.'

'Good try, but not good enough without unexplained cash

deposits in Weston's bank account.' Millson shook his head. 'No, I think they're a record of what was done to someone Weston hated, and he kept them to drool over later.' He picked up the foolscap envelope. 'Let's see what the inquiry agent's report has to say.'

As Millson pulled the stiff cover of the report from the envelope a photograph fell to the table. He picked it up and stared at it. 'What d'you make of this, Norris?' he asked, handing it to Scobie.

Scobie gave a whistle of surprise. 'It's Richard and Drusilla Layton digging a grave!' He looked at the photograph closely. 'From their ages I'd say this was taken around the time Katrina disappeared.' He looked at Millson. 'This is incredible!'

'Don't get excited,' Millson said. 'You don't imagine they'd pose for a picture of them burying her, do you?'

'Well, what else could it be? Look at the size and shape of the bundle. It's far too big for a dog,' Scobie said. 'And those two are capable of anything.'

'Being capable is not the same as doing,' Millson snapped. 'Go and persuade someone to make tea while I read the report.'

Millson had finished reading when Scobie returned with two cups of tea. He passed the report to Scobie. 'Your turn, Norris and I'd like a considered opinion when you've finished.' Millson sat back and sipped his tea.

Scobie began reading, pausing now and again to distil his thoughts. In Rory Grant's report of his visit to Julia Dean in Ridgewell he had not said the photograph showed Rick and Drusilla burying Katrina Kovacs, only that the large black bundle beside a recently dug hole seemed odd, and the position of the grave corresponded with a footprint he'd seen in the cement of the garage floor.

Scobie finished reading and said cautiously, 'Well, ob-

viously the photo was taken around the time Katrina disappeared and shows Rick and Drusilla in the act of burying
something the size of a human body. The inquiry agent
wonders how much of Julia Dean's wanderings were fantasy
and how much true. It's a good point because this information, including the photo, stems from her and she's the mad
granny Drusilla told me about the first time we met. It would
help if we knew who took the photo and why her granny's got
it.'

'It would also help if we knew what Harry Weston made of
all this when he read it,' Millson said. 'Anyway, we certainly
need to hear Rick and Drusilla Layton's explanations of the
photo. Make an appointment with them, but don't mention
what it's about, and make sure we see them together again like
last time. I don't want them agreeing their story in advance.'

'Shouldn't we ask Constance Layton about the photo first?
After all, it was her house and Rick and Drusilla were children
then.'

'And now they're old enough to answer for themselves,'
Millson said firmly.

131

Fifteen

As on the previous occasion, Richard and Drusilla Layton were already waiting when Amy showed Millson and Scobie into the front room of Hawkhills next morning.

'Will you have coffee, Chief Inspector?' Drusilla asked.

'Thank you, no,' Millson said.

She gave Amy a dismissive nod. 'Your sergeant wouldn't say why you wanted to see us. Is it about Katrina?'

'That, and the murder of Harry Weston,' Millson said.

'Hang on,' said Richard Layton. 'Our only connection with Harry was that Drusilla painted his wife's portrait, and I was thinking of merging my company with his.'

Millson reached into his pocket. 'Yes, but you see, Mr Weston had this photo of you and your cousin in his safe. Perhaps you'd explain it to us,' he said, handing it to him.

Rick glanced at the photo. 'Oh, that.' He smiled and passed it to Drusilla. 'Harry phoned me about it. He thought it showed Dru and me burying Katrina's body, would you believe? Said he was worried about joining me in business if there was something suspicious lurking in my background.'

'When was this?'

'About ten days before he was killed. I told him he was being silly and if he liked to come over I could soon put his mind at rest.'

While he was speaking Drusilla had gone to a large glazed

132

bookcase against the wall. She returned with a photo album which she opened and handed to Millson.

'The photo was taken at Aphrodite's funeral, Chief Inspector. Aphrodite was my dog. A Great Dane. She was magnificent . . . stood two foot six high and weighed eleven stone.'

'We gave her a great send off,' Rick added. 'It was quite an occasion.'

Millson and Scobie gazed at the double-page spread of photos. In the first ones Rick was dressed as a priest in long robes and stiff collar and Drusilla wore mourning clothes with hat and veil. Later photos showed them in trousers and gumboots, posing as grave-diggers. The other people present seemed more like onlookers than mourners. Scobie studied the faces. The only one he recognised was Constance Layton, Drusilla's mother.

'I don't see Katrina there,' he said.

'That's because she'd left Hawkhills by then,' Drusilla told him.

'How did the dog die?' asked Millson.

Her expression hardened. 'Julia, my grandmother, fed her chicken bones. You should never give a dog chicken bones. They splinter when the dog crunches them and the spikes perforate their insides. I had to have Aphrodite put down.' Drusilla reached out for a box of cigarettes on a nearby coffee table, took one out and lit it. 'I adored that dog. I never forgave granny.'

'Who took the photos?'

'She did. I made her . . . as a punishment.' She saw Millson raise his eyebrows. 'She knew – everyone knew – I was the only one allowed to feed Aphrodite.'

'But didn't she have some kind of mental problem?'

'Not at that time,' Drusilla said coldly. 'That was later.'

'I see.' Millson turned to Richard Layton. 'So, what was Mr Weston's reaction when you showed him these pictures?'

'He couldn't apologise quickly enough. Said he was relieved and reassured.'

'What happens now he's dead? Does the business pass to his wife?'

'I imagine so, but she's too upset to discuss business at the moment.'

'What's the relationship between you and Mrs Weston?'

'A business one, of course,' Rick said. 'She owns half Harry's company.'

'You're sure it's not closer than that?'

A slight smile hovered around Rick Layton's mouth. Yvonne had phoned him in a panic the day after Harry's murder, begging him not to reveal their affair. 'I've already denied it to the police,' she told him. 'I didn't want them thinking I might have killed Harry because of that. If you deny it too, there's no way they can prove anything.'

'Quite sure,' Rick told Millson. 'We're simply potential business partners.'

Millson let it pass. 'There were some other photos in Mr Weston's safe you might be able to help us with.' He signalled to Scobie who took the polaroids from his case and handed them to Layton. 'Do you happen to know where these were taken?'

Rick examined them one by one then passed them to Drusilla. 'I'm afraid not,' he said, although he was fairly sure he knew. Drusilla finished looking at them and, with a shake of her head, handed them back to Scobie.

'And just for the record,' Millson said, 'Where were you both between six and nine o'clock last Wednesday? That's the evening Mr Weston was murdered.'

Richard Layton answered. 'We were here. Together.'

'Anyone to confirm that?'

'No, Amy had the evening off. I think she went to the cinema.'

Millson nodded. 'Well, thank you both for your help.' He stood up. 'Oh, just one more thing. I'd like to take a look in your garage to see where Aphrodite was buried.'

Rick Layton's eyebrows rose. 'Sure, if you want to.'

They all trooped down the drive and as the electronically operated doors to the garage lifted, Drusilla strode ahead and inside. 'This is where Aphrodite is, Chief Inspector. Her head's right here.' She tapped the ground with her foot. In the concrete floor of the garage he saw the imprint of a shoe. 'I marked it myself,' she said.

'That's where the old inspection pit was,' Rick explained. 'In grandfather's time they had a chauffeur and mechanic to look after the cars. It made a good grave. We half-filled it with earth, put Aphrodite in then filled the rest with hard core and cemented it over.'

Millson nodded. 'Thank you. That seems to clear things up.'

'Layton lied about his relationship with Weston's wife,' Millson said as he drove out through the gate. 'And we only have his version of Harry Weston's visit. Maybe he lied about that too.'

'Well, Layton and the wife had good reasons to want Weston dead,' Scobie pointed out. 'She wanted to be rid of a husband she hated, and he wanted to get his hands on the business.'

'It's also possible Weston threatened him and Drusilla with something more than the photograph and they killed him to shut him up.'

'What though?' Scobie asked. 'What could Harry Weston know about Katrina's disappearance that we don't?'

'Perhaps that she never left Hawkhills.' Millson made a wry face. 'And I did know, or at least suspected it. Now I've seen those photos of the dog's funeral I'm certain of it.'

'You've lost me,' Scobie said.

'That business with the taxi . . . Katrina leaving with her suitcase and a man . . . it was a charade, a hoax. Don't you see? It was Drusilla and Richard Layton.' As Scobie gaped he went on, 'Remember Vy Rawlings telling us how they wowed the locals with their amateur dramatics? And remember how you and Kathy didn't recognise Dena in *Twelfth Night*? And now the dog funeral. If you hadn't known in advance, would you have recognised the priest and the woman in mourning as Rick and Drusilla?'

Scobie looked stunned. He said slowly, 'It's incredible . . . but yes, I can see it . . . you're right.' His expression changed. 'You don't think—' He stopped.

'What, Norris?'

'Well, that the dog's funeral was another hoax. Suppose Katrina was already dead and they switched bodies somehow?'

Millson shook his head. 'I know you believe them capable of anything, Norris, but they're not magicians.'

As Millson suspected, there had been more to Harry Weston's visit than Rick Layton had told him.

'I hear the police are investigating the disappearance of an au pair from Hawkhills,' Harry Weston had said. 'And I have this photo of you and Drusilla burying a body in your garage around the time she disappeared.'

Rick Layton was silent for a moment. Then, opening his desk drawer he pressed the 'record' button on the tape recorder linked to the phone.

'What are you implying, Harry?' He injected a note of anxiety into his tone.

'Nothing. I was wondering whether to send it to the police. And then I'm thinking, why cause trouble for a man who wants to do business with me?'

'Get to the point, Harry. What do you want?'

'Well, the way I see things you're not offering nearly enough for my half of the business.'

'I see. That sounds like blackmail to me.'

'Call it what you like, but you can't expect me to do business with a man who has a dodgy background like yours. Unless the price is attractive and reflects the risk, of course. I think we need to discuss this, don't you?'

'Yes, all right.'

When Weston reached Hawkhills Rick Layton met him halfway down the drive and took him into the garage. 'In here Harry,' he said. 'I don't want to worry Drusilla. This is between you and me.'

Harry followed him warily past the black Mercedes and Drusilla's Porsche to where there was the mark of a shoeprint in the floor. Rick pointed. 'That's where the body is, Harry. That's where we buried Drusilla's dog.' He opened the boot of the Porsche and took out the album of photos. 'Take a look for yourself.'

Harry scanned them. 'All right,' he said. 'I accept you weren't burying Katrina.'

'Accept? You were trying to blackmail me, damn you! I recorded what you said on the phone.'

'That doesn't frighten me. I'll simply send the photo to the police and put myself in the clear.'

'I'd rather you didn't. Not because we've done anything wrong but because it would upset Drusilla's mother and grandmother if the police started questioning them. Look, Harry, there's no sense in being enemies, and I'm willing to pay a good price for your company. How much do you want?'

Richard Layton's friendliness convinced Harry Weston there was more to this au pair inquiry than he'd thought. Rick didn't want the police questioning Drusilla's batty granny, that was obvious. Which meant there must be more to be got from her, and a great deal more to be squeezed from Rick Layton than a few thousand extra for Harry's computing company.

'I'd like to think about that, Rick. Give me a few days to talk to my accountant and I'll come up with a figure.'

He knew from the expression on Rick Layton's face he'd been right.

Rory Grant was apprehensive when he picked Amy up outside Hawkhills. 'I've got the day off Sunday,' she'd told him on the phone. 'They'll be out on their boat all day. I want to put some flowers on granddad's grave. Will you take me?'

It was the first time they'd spoken since he'd phoned her to confirm Yvonne Weston's identity. It had been the day before Mrs Weston's husband was found murdered. Rory worried that his information had triggered the killing because Mr Hersham had told the husband about his wife's affair at midday and he was murdered the same evening. After that, Rory had put off explaining to Amy why he wanted to know about Mrs Weston, as he'd promised, and now he was in a quandary. She hadn't mentioned the murder on the phone and her voice had sounded unfriendly.

Amy was carrying flowers from Hawkhills freshly cut for her by the gardener. She was solemn-faced and silent on the journey to the cemetery, and Rory thought it best not to say anything about the murder until she brought up it up herself.

Bert Foster's grave now had a headstone and when Amy had finished arranging the flowers in the vase in front of it Rory broke the long silence between them.

'He was quite old, wasn't he?' he said, noticing 'Aged 72' carved in the marble. He intended that to be comforting but Amy rounded on him.

'You don't miss someone less because they're old,' she

snapped. 'And, anyway, I don't know how old he really was. I just guessed.'

'I'm sorry, I didn't mean—'

'Don't sorry me,' she said angrily. 'You're a rotten slimy creep! Getting round me to tell you about Rick and Drusilla and everything.'

'Amy, let me explain. I—'

'I don't want your miserable excuses!' she said furiously. 'After that poor woman's husband was murdered I checked up on you. You're not a reporter at all. You work for some scabby inquiry firm.'

'Yes, but I'm going to—'

'The only reason for seeing you today was to tell you what I thought of you. And now I've done it, I never want to see you again. So, take me home.'

'Amy . . . *please*—'

'Take me home!'

At the gates of Hawkhills, he made a last attempt. 'I love you, Amy,' he said, as she stepped out of the car.

She turned back. 'Don't come the softie with me. It won't work.' She got out and slammed the door. As he gazed at her pleadingly she stuck two fingers in the air at him and walked off.

Sixteen

Earlier that Sunday morning Rick and Drusilla had collected Elaine and Brian from their flat in Colchester and driven to Walton. At the yacht club there the party boarded Rick and Drusilla's luxury cruiser *Moon Rider* lying in the deep water pool. They seemed an oddly assorted foursome: Rick in immaculate white slacks, Drusilla, in navy-blue bell-bottomed trousers and Brian and Elaine in jeans and jumpers.

'We'll take a short sea trip and come back to Stone Point for lunch and a swim,' Rick said. He climbed to the flying bridge and started the engines while Drusilla, with practised hands, tended the mooring ropes and cast off. Slowly, the big cruiser edged forward and over the sill at the pool gates into the creek beyond.

The day was warm and sunny, with a light wind, and the water was smooth as they glided through the moorings in Foundry Creek, along Walton channel and out through the buoyed channel to Island Point. Beyond the Island Point buoy Rick turned to Drusilla.

'You take over, Dru, while I take Elaine below and show her round.'

She nodded and mounted the padded helmsman's seat to take his place at the wheel. 'Come up here with me and try steering,' Drusilla said, motioning to Brian as Rick helped Elaine down the companionway.

She stood him in front of her, between her and the wheel so that he was half-sitting on her lap. For a while he gripped the wheel and stared ahead, becoming accustomed to the cruiser's response to alterations of the wheel.

'Faster,' Drusilla said, and reaching past him she opened the throttles. The bow lifted and the cruiser planed effortlessly over the sea towards Harwich. Her arms went round his waist, hugging him. 'Doesn't all this power excite you?' Her tongue licked his ear. 'I like you, little Teddy. You don't mind if I call you my little Teddy, do you?'

Politely, he shook his head. She nipped his ear with her teeth and laughed when he jumped. 'I used to bite my Teddy when I was a little girl,' she said.

Later, they returned to the Backwaters and dropped anchor by the sandy beach at Stone Point. On the sun deck Drusilla stripped off her jacket and trousers. Underneath she wore a red two-piece costume. Climbing over the lifelines, she poised briefly and dived in.

'I should use the bathing platform at the stern, if I were you,' Rick advised Brian and Elaine when they appeared in swimming costumes. 'And watch the current. The tide is very strong here.'

Cautiously, Brian and Elaine lowered themselves into the water from the bathing platform and splashed out for the shore. Behind them Rick plunged in and overtook them in a racing crawl.

After the swim they returned to the boat and Drusilla opened the food hamper and laid the table on the afterdeck. Rick brought champagne from the fridge in an ice-bucket and filled the glasses.

'What shall we drink to?' he asked, handing them round.

'Ourselves, of course,' said Drusilla.

'Ourselves, then.' He raised his glass.

Drusilla threaded her arm through Brian's and brought the

glass back to her lips. 'To us,' she said. Her face close to his, the hazel eyes glowed.

'To us,' Brian repeated.

Rick put his mouth to Elaine's ear. 'To a very pretty girl,' he whispered. She smiled and looked away.

They remained at anchor, the champagne flowing, and by mid-afternoon Brian and Elaine were drunk.

'Are you game for a sail, Brian?' asked Drusilla.

'Of course,' he said belligerently.

'OK. Let's get wet suits on then.' She turned to Rick. 'Launch the Laser for us.' She looked at Elaine slumped in a deckchair and murmured, 'If you can't be good be careful, Rick.'

A short while after, as the racing dinghy disappeared from view in Hamford Water, Rick guided an unsteady Elaine down the companionway to the stateroom below.

When Drusilla and Brian returned an hour later Rick and Elaine were lying on the beach, sunbathing. Drusilla waved, tied up the dinghy and mounted the boarding ladder. Brian, clumsy in a wet suit, followed.

In the forecabin Drusilla stripped off her wet suit. Underneath she was wearing the red two-piece costume, the bottom a mere scrap of material secured with tie-cords at the sides. She watched Brian wrestling with the heavy zip of his wet suit.

'Here, let me help.' With strong expert fingers she unzipped him from neck to crotch. Then, with a smile, she pulled the tie-cords of her costume and dropped it on the floor. She stepped forward and, much taller than him, had to bend her head to put her mouth to his. She cupped her hands behind his head, lips brushing his, then suddenly forced them apart with her tongue and slid it deep into his mouth. He clutched her to avoid overbalancing as the pulsating tip explored deeper. Then suddenly he broke from her and thrust her violently away.

142

'What on earth's the matter with you?' she asked furiously. 'Are you gay or something?' She jumped back as his eyes flashed murderously.

'No, I'm bloody not!' he said through his teeth.

'What then?' she demanded.

'Nothing,' he said sulkily. 'I'm not in the mood.'

'Oh, really?' she said mockingly. 'More like no balls.'

That's when I thought he was going to knife me, she told Rick later. He actually reached for the knife at his belt.

It was dark when they moored *Moon Rider* in the pool and drove away. There was little conversation on the drive to Colchester. Brian, tired and sober, was confused. The wanton creature who'd devoured him earlier sat calm and unruffled in the front seat beside her cousin. Next to Brian, Elaine lolled in the corner of the car, half asleep.

When they reached Brian and Elaine's flat the goodbyes were restrained, the parting of casual acquaintances. 'Would you like to come in for a coffee?' Elaine asked politely.

Drusilla shook her head. 'Another time, perhaps.'

'It was a lovely day,' Brian said. 'Thanks for everything.'

'Not at all. We enjoyed it too,' Rick called out as he reversed the Mercedes and drove away.

Drusilla took a cigarette from a packet in the glove compartment and lit it from the dashboard lighter. She snuggled down in her seat, laying her blonde head on her cousin's shoulder.

'How was your day, Dru?' he asked.

Her brow wrinkled. 'Interesting, very interesting. I was miffed with Brian after the evening they came to dinner. This time I was determined to open him up. And I did.' She related the incident in the forecabin. 'The burglary Elaine told you about was a lot more serious than she said. The thugs attacked Brian and practically neutered him.'

'That was no burglary,' Rick said. 'That was Harry's way of

taking revenge.' He told her how Brian Hall had nearly succeeded in destroying Harry Weston's business. 'The bastard must have hired some heavies to beat him up and wreck his home. The polaroids the police showed us were Harry's souvenirs.'

'Poor little Brian,' she said.

'And Elaine,' said Rick.

'Mm.' She nuzzled him affectionately. 'She's a little cutie. Did you have her today?'

He shrugged. 'Not really.'

Drusilla raised her head from his shoulder to look at him. His face was a pale blur in the dim glow of the dashboard. 'It's not like you to fail, darling.'

'I didn't try,' he muttered. 'She's a nice girl. We talked about her marriage. She's very unhappy.'

Drusilla stared at him for a long moment. Then looked away from him and out of the window, frowning hard.

It was Monday morning and Millson was depressed. The result of the house-to-house inquiries about Harry Weston's murder and the public appeal had been disappointing. The house was in a residential area and the cars so far identified driving along the street between six and nine p.m. had all belonged to local residents. Harry Weston had been seen arriving home just after half-past five, and his wife, Yvonne, half an hour after him. No one had been seen entering or leaving the house after Yvonne left again a quarter of an hour later.

Yvonne Weston's statement of her movements after leaving the house had been checked. Her friend, Janet, confirmed Yvonne phoned her about six thirty to say she was unwell and couldn't keep their date at the theatre; and the George hotel had confirmed Yvonne booked in at eight o'clock, as she said.

An examination of Harry Weston's bank statements and

correspondence had revealed nothing untoward, and the phone calls made from the house in the days leading up to his death had all seemed to be normal social or business calls.

While George Millson was gloomily reviewing the case there was a knock on the door and a DC entered.

'A new witness, sir. Sounds promising. Says he saw someone at the Westons' house late in the evening.'

'Wheel him in then,' Millson said cheerfully, banging on his wall to summon Scobie from next door.

Mr Pettifer was a City businessman who lived opposite to the Westons' house in Kelvedon. He explained that very early on the morning Harry Weston's body was discovered he'd departed on a business trip to New York and had only just returned and learned of his murder.

'So, what have you to tell us, Mr Pettifer?' Millson asked.

'The newspaper reports say Mr Weston was killed between six and nine o'clock the night before, Chief Inspector. Well, I saw someone coming out of his house at a quarter to nine that night.'

Millson's eyes lit up. 'You're sure of the time?'

'Oh, absolutely. I was taking my wife's dog for a pee and there was a programme on telly I wanted to see at nine, so I was keeping an eye on the time.'

Scobie took out his pen. 'Can you give us a description of this person please, Mr Pettifer?'

'Unfortunately, it was dark and there was a slight drizzle so I couldn't see very well. And, of course, I had no reason to take much notice then,' he said apologetically.

'Just do the best you can,' Millson said. 'Start from when you first saw the person.'

'Right. I was opening my gate, the dog was on the lead, and what caught my attention was the light from Mr Weston's front door when it opened and closed as someone came out. I can't say whether it was a man or a woman but—' He stopped. 'I've just thought. There was no one at the door saying goodbye, letting this person out, so . . .'

'It was very probably his killer.' Millson finished the sentence for him.

'Oh.' Mr Pettifer looked anxious. 'This is important then.'

'Very important,' Millson said. 'So, continue with what you saw, please.'

Mr Pettifer's forehead creased as he half-closed his eyes and recalled the scene. 'This figure had on a dark-coloured rain-coat . . . pulled up the hood as soon as they felt the drizzle . . . walked quickly down the path and off along the street towards the main road.'

'Were the lights on in the rest of the house?' Millson asked.

'No, well not in the front, anyway. Only the hall light.'

'What sort of build was this person?' Scobie asked. 'Tall, short, fat, thin?'

'I didn't really notice. But not fat, though.' Mr Pettifer shook his head helplessly. 'I haven't been much help, have I?'

'On the contrary,' Millson assured him, 'You've been a great deal of help. And if you remember anything more, give us a ring straight away.'

When Scobie returned from escorting Mr Pettifer to the front door Millson said, 'Bring Yvonne Weston in for questioning, Norris. I expect she'll come voluntarily but if not, arrest her on suspicion of being involved in her husband's murder. And make sure you caution her properly.'

Yvonne Weston had come in willingly but she was pale-faced and anxious when she faced Millson and Scobie across the table in the Interview Room. Her anxiety increased when Millson told her the interview would be recorded, and Scobie switched on the machine. Millson had discussed tactics with Scobie beforehand. They would start with trying to get an admission of her relationship with Layton and then go over her movements on the evening of the murder again. If she stood by her story they would challenge her with returning to the house later and leaving again at nine o'clock.

'Thank you for coming in, Mrs Weston,' Millson began. 'I want to ask you again about the relationship between you and Richard Layton. Do you still maintain you weren't lovers?'

'I do. And I'm sure Mr Layton will confirm it,' she said.

'Yes, he already has,' said Millson. 'But were you aware your husband engaged a private inquiry agency to investigate him?'

'Oh, yes. Harry told me himself. He wanted to check Rick's business and financial standing.'

'The inquiry went wider than that, Mrs Weston.' Millson gave Scobie a nod.

Scobie opened a folder. 'This is what the inquiry agent says, Mrs Weston.' Scobie read from John Hersham's letter to Millson. 'Mrs Weston and Mr Layton were seen kissing and embracing and then went upstairs to bed.'

'This is ridiculous!' Yvonne said angrily. 'Rick often gave me a kiss, and only someone with a dirty mind would assume a man and woman going upstairs in a house meant they were going to bed.'

'There's more,' Scobie said, and continued reading. 'On another occasion Mr Layton took Mrs Weston down to the studio at the bottom of the garden. Shortly after there were sounds of them having sex. They were in there for about an hour.'

Yvonne's eyes widened in shock. 'Have you asked me here just to listen to this muck, Chief Inspector?

'No, I want to discover the truth,' Millson said. 'Your husband was murdered following a quarrel between you. It's clear to me the quarrel was over your relationship with Richard Layton. Now, if you continue to deny it I'll obtain a sworn statement from the original witness and charge you with obstructing a police investigation. Do you want that?'

Her head drooped and she sat looking at her hands. 'No,' she said after a moment and looked up. 'Yes, all right. I had sex with Rick. *He* wanted my help with persuading Harry to agree to a merger, and *I* wanted *him*. It was as simple as that.' She looked Millson in the eyes. 'And no, I didn't care a fig for Harry and I'll take good sex wherever I can find it,' she said defiantly.

Millson nodded. 'That's very frank of you, Mrs Weston.'

'Can I go now?'

'I'm afraid not. A new witness has come forward. But first, I want to go over what you told us of your movements that evening and give you the chance to correct anything you said.' He nodded to Scobie again.

Scobie turned back some pages in his notebook. 'According to you, Mrs Weston, you returned home at five forty-five and left again soon after six following a quarrel with your husband. You phoned your friend, Janet Brown, about six-thirty and told her you didn't feel like going to the theatre that evening. Then you drove around for a while because you felt upset, and later booked in to the George hotel. The reception clerk confirms this was at eight o'clock.'

Millson leaned forward and put his arms on the table. 'Are those movements and times correct, Mrs Weston?'

'Yes, they are.'

'Did you go out again after booking in at the hotel?'

'No, I stayed in my room. I was exhausted. I had room service bring me a meal about ten o'clock and then I went to bed.'

'You didn't have second thoughts and return home to try and reason with Harry? Patch things up, perhaps?'

'No, I'd finished with him. There was no question of patching things up.'

'All right, let's go back to when you arrived home that day. We know the inquiry agency phoned your husband at his office around three o'clock that afternoon and told him about your affair with Rick Layton. Harry must have driven straight home to confront you with it. He was probably in a rage. A middle-aged man whose wife has taken a younger lover. There's a violent quarrel during which he picks up a knife and slashes your portrait.' He glanced at Yvonne Weston. She was sitting with her head bowed, listening intently. 'It's your story of what happened after that I find difficult to accept,' he went on. 'I simply can't believe Harry calmly stood by and watched you walk out. I think he tried to stop you, perhaps threatened you with the same knife. There was a struggle and you stabbed him. In self defence, perhaps,' he added, offering her a route to a confession.

She looked up. 'No. There was no struggle and I didn't stab him. I keep telling you, he was alive when I left the house.'

'OK. We'll go along with that then. You fled soon after he started on you, demanding explanations. A witness says you looked agitated and left in a hurry. Then, later that evening, after booking in at the hotel, you returned to have it out with him and *that's* when you had the quarrel and he slashed your picture.'

'No, the quarrel started the moment I got home. I did *not* go back to the house again,' she said firmly.

'The other possibility,' Millson went on, as though she hadn't spoken. 'Is that you killed him before you left the house the first time. Then, realising you'd be a suspect, you decided to return and stage a break-in and burglary to make it appear he'd been killed by an intruder.'

'NO! And you can't keep saying I went back to the house just because I can't prove I didn't leave the hotel.'

'There's another reason for saying it, Mrs Weston. A new witness has come forward who saw someone come out of the front door of your house at a quarter to nine that evening. I believe that someone was you.'

'No! No, it wasn't!' she said desperately.

'Who else could it have been?'

She lowered her eyes. 'I don't know.'

Millson remained silent, deliberately letting the time pass to increase tension. After a while he said gently, 'I don't think you realise the seriousness of your situation, Yvonne. And I can't help you unless you tell me the truth.'

She continued looking down at the table. Millson and Scobie remained still . . . waiting. At last she said quietly, 'It wasn't like you said.'

Millson felt the familiar relief that came at this point in an interview. Keeping his voice level he said, 'Then tell me how it was.'

She swallowed and raised her head. 'After Harry slashed the picture he put down the knife and came towards me. He called me names . . . said he was going to teach me a lesson. I ran and grabbed the knife, and told him to keep away. But he just laughed and kept coming. I shouted I'd kill him if he touched me, and I raised the knife.' She let out her breath. 'I think he suddenly realised I meant it, and I was about to stick the knife in him, because he stopped and backed off.' She looked Millson full in the face. 'And I *did* mean it. I *would* have killed him.' She looked away. 'After that he didn't try to stop me leaving. I didn't kill Harry, Chief Inspector, I swear I didn't. And I didn't go back to the house later.'

Her violet eyes met his again, pleading and appealing. Millson was unmoved. Yvonne Weston's account of what happened sounded sincere, but he'd encountered other eyes like that. On two occasions they'd belonged to cold-hearted killers.

'This knife you were going to stab him with, Yvonne. What sort of knife was it?'

'A carving knife, the one Harry attacked the picture with.'

Not the murder weapon then. 'Just two more questions,' he said. 'I asked you to check if anything was missing from the house, especially kitchen knives. Did you do that?'

'Yes. As far as I can see there's nothing at all missing, and all my kitchen knives are still there.'

'And what happens to your husband's business now he's dead?'

'It belongs to me, along with the house and everything else.'

Millson nodded. 'Thank you, Mrs Weston. After you've signed a formal statement of what you've said to me you'll be free to go.'

After she left Millson phoned the press liaison officer and dictated an urgent appeal for the person seen leaving Harry Weston's house around nine o'clock on the night of the murder to come forward. He didn't expect a response. It was a precaution against there being an innocent explanation for the caller Mr Pettifer had seen.

Next, he asked Scobie to make an appointment to call on Richard Layton.

Seventeen

Richard Layton was impatient when they arrived at Hawkhills. 'I hope this won't take long, Chief Inspector. I've had to put off a meeting to be here.'

'It'll take as long as it takes you to give truthful answers to my questions, Mr Layton,' Millson told him brusquely. 'You lied to me about your relationship with Harry Weston's wife.'

'Oh, that.' Layton clicked his tongue in irritation. 'I didn't lie. I said it was a business one and it was.' Yvonne had warned him she'd confessed when the police questioned her this time. 'I wanted her signature on a contract, and she made it clear her price for it was sex with me. I paid and that's business so far as I'm concerned. And if you think we're lovers and killed Harry so we could be together, you couldn't be more wrong.'

'I'm looking at the situation from a different angle, Mr Layton. Mr Weston's company was in joint names. Now he's dead it passes to his wife and she can negotiate her own deal with you. So, she's rid of a husband she obviously hated, and you get the business you wanted. Which means his death was very convenient for both of you, particularly if he was refusing to surrender his half of the business.'

'He wasn't refusing. He'd agreed.'

'There's no proof of that, though,' Millson said. 'All there is among his papers is an unsigned contract.'

'He hadn't signed because he wanted to consult his accountant first.' Angrily, Rick went on, 'It's outrageous of you to suggest Yvonne and I killed Harry!'

'I didn't. I said his death was very convenient,' Millson said mildly. 'Let me turn to something else. When Harry Weston phoned about that photo of you and Drusilla in the garage, why didn't you explain you were burying a dog? Why bring him here to look at an album of photographs?'

'Because he wouldn't have taken my word for it.'

'Really?' Millson's tone was sceptical. 'I've read the inquiry agent's report on his visit to Drusilla's grandmother.' Millson saw Rick Layton's eyes flinch. 'And what it says might well have given Harry Weston reason to believe he could threaten you and Drusilla about Katrina's disappearance.'

'That's absurd. How could he when we had nothing to do with it? Dru and I weren't even here when she left. Constance had taken us to the beach that day.'

'What time did you leave?'

'For heaven's sake, it was a long time ago. I don't recall exactly. About nine or ten o'clock, I think.'

'And who was left in the house?'

'Just Katrina. Dru's grandmother was staying with us, but she'd returned to her own house for a couple of days and hadn't arrived back. She turned up later, just as Katrina was leaving.'

The silly old woman had nearly ruined the whole scene, Rick recalled. Everything had been working well until her untimely arrival. Fourteen-year-old Drusilla had gone in to Katrina's flat and hunted through drawers and cupboards, selecting garments. She'd stripped off her own clothes and put on Katrina's, padding them with towels and layers of underwear to make them fit and to give herself a fuller figure. Tucking her fair hair under a skull cap, she donned an auburn wig from their props cupboard, and sat down at the dressing-table with her make-up box. When she'd finished she inserted a wad of cotton wool inside each cheek, pulled on a pair of boots with three-inch heels, and stood up. She turned to Rick.

'How do I look?'

He studied her carefully. 'Fine. A bit fat round the tum, though.'

'That's because she's preggers.'

'But she wasn't.'

'I know that, dummy. But anyone who sees us will think she was and that's why she left secretly.' She took another look at herself in a full-length mirror then turned to him again. 'Now let's see what we can do with you.'

Half an hour later he'd phoned for a taxi and when it arrived they emerged from the house carrying suitcases. Rick now had a moustache and wore an overcoat and suit belonging to Drusilla's father. His head was covered with a cap pulled low over his forehead.

'You for the station?' the driver asked.

They nodded, opened the car boot and put in their suitcases. That was the moment they saw Julia Dean's car about to turn into the other end of the drive. They jumped into the taxi and told the driver to drive on.

At Alresford station they bought tickets to Liverpool Street and caught the next train. When the train reached Colchester, a normal-looking Rick and Drusilla got off, wearing their own clothes again. They had carried them in the suitcases and changed in the toilet compartment on the journey from Alresford.

Rick saw Millson eyeing him. 'That's how we know Katrina left in a taxi with a man.'

'Quite so.' Millson nodded. 'Would you mind showing me where Katrina was living while she was at Hawkhills?'

'Not at all. She lived in the annexe.' He stood up. 'It's this way.'

They followed him across the hall and into the kitchen.

Amy was at the sink. 'Amy, these two gentlemen would like to look at the annexe,' he told her. 'You don't mind, do you?'

'No, that's OK.' Amy was subdued, wondering if the policemen knew she was the one who'd given the information about Mrs Weston. There had been a terrible scene about that with Drusilla yesterday evening after Mrs Weston had phoned Rick and told him an inquiry agent had given a detailed account of their meetings to the police.

Drusilla had stormed into the kitchen as Amy was preparing the evening meal. 'You've been talking to some private eye about Rick and Yvonne,' she said furiously.

'I didn't know that's what—'

'After all I've done for you.' Drusilla's mouth turned an ugly shape. 'What did he do to loosen your tongue? Give you money? Or did he French you in the back of his car?'

'Stop it!' Amy cried, her eyes filling with tears. 'I'm sorry! I didn't understand.'

'If you open your pretty little mouth again I'll put you out on the street. Do you understand?'

Amy nodded dumbly, tears coursing down her cheeks. Drusilla watched her for a while. Then her face softened and she stepped forward and took the sobbing girl in her arms. 'You silly goose, letting him seduce you,' she murmured, stroking Amy's hair.

Rick Layton opened the door leading to the annexe and stood aside for Millson and Scobie to enter the small hallway beyond. 'It's self-contained,' he said. 'Bedroom, bathroom and sitting-room.'

As Millson and Scobie stepped forward into the bedroom, he hung back. He hadn't been in there since the night it happened. He heard Millson's voice and smothered the memory.

'This place is like a prison,' Millson called out. 'Why are there bars on the inside of the windows?'

Rick relaxed. 'Constance had them put in five or six years ago. Drusilla's grandmother was living with us permanently then and she had a habit of wandering off and causing trouble. Locking her in didn't work because she'd climb out of the window in the middle of the night. One time she set fire to the barn here. That was when Constance had her committed to Ridgewell.'

'I see.' Millson returned to the hallway and said casually, 'Remarkable performers you and your cousin were as children. Those photos of the dog's funeral were amazing. And I gather from Mrs Rawlings you used to give shows for the locals.' He saw Rick Layton's mouth twitch and the sudden change in his expression. 'I'm impressed,' Millson said.

'Yes, I suppose we were pretty good,' Rick said uneasily. 'I don't see what this has to do with your inquiry, though.'

'Nor do I at the moment,' Millson said cheerfully. He was now certain Rick and Drusilla had faked Katrina's departure from Hawkhills but, without direct evidence, there was no point in pursuing it.

That lunchtime Rick Layton met Elaine Hall at the yacht club in Walton. It was a meeting she'd agreed to last Sunday on board *Moon Rider*.

After her marriage, Elaine had tried to adjust to Brian's idiosyncrasies and the clockwork regularity of his lovemaking. She told herself she was a lucky girl. She had a nice home and a kind husband and it was unreasonable to expect to have everything you wanted in life. She had nearly half, and that was more than most people had. She would have liked a baby, but Brian told her not for three years. That was when it was scheduled for on his events timetable. It was the only thing he refused her, and it might have saved her from Rick Layton.

At first, when Rick took her in his arms in *Moon Rider's* stateroom, she had turned her head away and made a hurried excuse. 'I'm sorry. I don't know what's the matter with me. I think I've had too much to drink.'

He raised her chin and looked into her eyes. 'It's not the drink,' he said. 'You're unhappy. I can see it in your eyes.'

'Don't be kind. You'll make me feel worse.'

The tremor in her voice brought back the memory of their kiss in the garden at Hawkhills. He bent forward to kiss her soft mouth again.

'No, please don't,' she begged.

'Don't tell me you love your husband?'

She lowered her head without answering. He tried to tilt her face up and she turned away. 'Brian's just outside on deck.'

'Meaning if he weren't, you would?'

'That's unfair. Couldn't we just talk?' she pleaded.

He was contrite. 'Yes, of course. I'm being an insensitive idiot.'

Later he'd told her, 'You mustn't take life so seriously. What you need is cheering up. Let's meet for lunch.' That was when she'd made the date with him.

She felt a tingle of excitement as she parked her powder-blue Mini and saw him waiting for her on the yacht club veranda. He came down the steps towards her.

'You're very lovely,' he said.

'Thank you.' She felt herself blushing.

He smiled. There was an innocence about Elaine Hall that intrigued him. He took her arm and guided her into the lounge bar of the club. It was empty. She went to the windows and gazed out.

'It looks so peaceful. Aren't the Backwaters over there somewhere?'

'Yes, you can see them better from the upstairs balcony. There's a telescope up there.'

On the balcony Elaine fiddled with the telescope, finding it difficult to focus. Rick bent over her to help. Elaine's nearness and her long eyelashes and soft cheeks aroused a familiar urge. He brushed the side of her neck with his lips. She pretended not to notice and concentrated on locating the Twizzle and Horsey Island. His hands went round her waist and as she lifted her head from the eyepiece, he turned her towards him.

It was a long kiss. When it ended and he gazed down at her parted lips and closed eyes, he found her vulnerability unbearable. Abruptly, he turned and led her downstairs.

'I thought we might have a pre-lunch drink on *Moon Rider*,' he said. Satan . . . tempting . . . nudging. 'Or would you prefer a drink at the bar here?' Now offering the angel a chance to escape her fall from grace.

'Oh, I'd love to see *Moon Rider* again,' the angel said eagerly.

They crossed the gravelled car park and walked along the embankment to where *Moon Rider* was berthed, stern-to to the bank, in the deep water pool. The cruiser lay, sleek and powerful, the mirror-finish of the dark hull reflecting in the still water.

'She's beautiful,' the angel breathes, one foot poised on the gangplank, a hand resting on the rail.

He nods and the angel turns and steps onwards along the gangplank. Satan follows a pace behind.

In the stateroom the angel turns, looks up into the blue eyes and moves, fatally, into his arms. Satan presses hardness against softness and the sensuous mouth descends. Her eyelids flutter briefly then close as she surrenders herself to the coming storm.

Moments earlier, Drusilla's silver Porsche had sped along the private road to the club. She had been commissioned to paint a watercolour of the creeks at low tide. As she parked in front of the clubhouse she noticed her cousin's black Mercedes and the powder-blue Mini beside it. She frowned, and looking across to the pool saw him and Elaine stepping on board *Moon Rider*. She watched them enter the stateroom and, through the windows, saw them embrace. Then the door into the bow section, which was mostly taken up by a triangular-shaped foam mattress, opened and closed behind them. Drusilla waited, willing them to come out again. Time passed and she sat immobile in her car, with a face that seemed carved in stone.

Then, with a last glance at the cruiser, she started the Porsche and roared away, gravel spitting from the skidding tyres.

Richard Layton phoned Millson next morning. 'I've been thinking about those polaroid photos Harry Weston had in his safe, Chief Inspector. I have an idea they were taken in the house of an employee of mine, Brian Hall, when he lived in London. He was burgled not long before he joined my staff and moved down here.'

'But why would Mr Weston have them?'

'Well, Brian did once work for him.' Let the police ferret out the rest for themselves.

'That's very interesting and thank you for the information,' Millson said. 'May I have his address?'

Rick gave him Brian Hall's address. 'I wouldn't like him to know his boss has been talking to the police about him, though. Not good for staff relations.'

'I'll respect your confidence, Mr Layton.'

Eighteen

B rian Hall and his wife lived in a rented bungalow in Marks Tey. 'Why should Harry Weston have photos of his employee's vandalised house?' Millson asked Scobie as they pulled up at the address that evening.

'The ones of the bedroom are pornographic, so perhaps he enjoyed looking at them,' Scobie suggested.

'Maybe, but there has to be another reason as well.'

Brian Hall seemed anxious as they identified themselves and Millson told him they were investigating the murder of Harold Weston. He showed them to a small sitting-room and when they were seated Scobie brought out the photos. 'We'd like you to look at these photos, Mr Hall, and tell us if you recognise them.'

Brian Hall's face froze with shock as he looked at them. *The bastard had taken photos! He'd been there . . . in the house . . . watching and listening.* He wondered what other information the police had. Handing the photos back he said cautiously, 'They seem to be photographs of our house in London after it was burgled.'

'When was this?' Scobie asked.

'A month ago.'

Brian said he'd come home from work one evening and been set upon as he stepped inside his front door. 'They wanted to know where the money was and when I said I didn't know what they were talking about, they started

160

beating me and tearing the place apart looking for it. Eventually, they realised they'd got the wrong man and the wrong house.'

'You say "they", Mr Hall. How many were there?' Scobie asked.

'Three.' *Two to hold him while the third* . . . Brian shut his mind to the memory.

'Can you explain how these photos came to be in Mr Weston's safe?' Millson asked.

'No, I can't. It's very strange,' Brian said. If they asked about the hacking, he would deny it. There was no way of proving it was him.

'I understand you used to work for Mr Weston at one time.'

'Yes, I did. For about six months. I left in March last year.' Brian's soft brown eyes gazed at him.

They reminded Millson of his ex-wife's King Charles Spaniel and he said abruptly, 'Thank you, Mr Hall. I'd like a word with your wife now.'

'She wasn't there when it happened, Chief Inspector, she was at her mother's. And those photos would upset her. No, I can't allow it.'

Millson said curtly, 'A man has been murdered, Mr Hall. Don't tell me what you can or can't allow. Fetch your wife, please.'

Brian glared at him then stood up and marched out of the door. He returned with Elaine and sat down again.

'Alone, if you don't mind,' Millson said and, seeing Hall about to argue, repeated forcefully, 'Alone, Mr Hall.' He wondered, from Brian's face as he left the room again, what raging emotions lay hidden behind those dog-like eyes.

He turned to Elaine, sitting primly on the edge of her seat. 'Your husband has been telling us about the unpleasant break-in at your previous address, Mrs Hall. I know you weren't present when it took place, but would you tell us what you found when you got home that night?'

'It was awful,' Elaine said in a quiet voice. 'Really horrible. Brian was lying in the hall. He was almost unconscious and the house had been wrecked.'

'What do you mean, "wrecked"?'

'The upholstery of the sofa and armchairs had been slashed, the television, hi-fi and video had been smashed and the floor was covered with broken glass and china.'

'Did you call the police?'

She looked uncomfortable. 'Brian wouldn't let me. He said it wouldn't do any good and he couldn't face the hassle and publicity. He wouldn't let me call an ambulance either. I didn't realise how badly he was hurt or I'd have done it anyway.' She said tearfully, 'Nothing showed, you see, and his face wasn't marked at all.'

Scobie looked up from taking notes. 'What injuries did he have, then?'

'There were no broken bones but when I helped him out of his clothes he was black and blue all over. They must have beaten him with rubber truncheons or something. He was in terrible pain.'

Scobie and Millson looked at each other. A professional job. 'Didn't you think this amount of violence was extreme for ordinary burglars, Mrs Hall?' Millson asked.

'Yes, but Brian explained it was a case of mistaken identity. They thought he had a lot of money and jewellery and they beat him up to make him tell where it was hidden. But he couldn't, of course, poor lamb.'

Millson reached for the polaroids. He picked out one taken of the bedroom and handed it to her. She stared at the photo, her eyes widening.

Elaine's clothes had been emptied from the wardrobe and

drawers, and her underwear strewn about the room. On the bed, one of her dresses was laid out with the skirt pulled up to display a pair of knickers and stockings, the stockings arranged with the legs apart and the feet inserted into a pair of high-heeled shoes on the floor. It was obvious what was being portrayed.

'This is what they did in the bedroom,' she said. 'It made me feel sick. Brian cried when he saw it.'

'I'm not surprised,' said Millson.

'But why did they do it?'

'It symbolises rape, Mrs Hall, that's why,' Millson told her.

'Oh, God!' She drew in her breath sharply.

'This was a very personal attack and intended to cripple your husband mentally and physically. Almost certainly perpetrated by someone with a dangerous grudge. Do you know who that might be?'

She looked scared. 'No, I can't think of anyone like that.'

'Thank you, Mrs Hall, and I'm sorry I had to put you through this. Would you ask your husband to come in again, please?'

She paused at the door. 'These men, are they . . . ?'

'You're not in any danger now,' he assured her.

When Hall entered and sat down, Millson said irritably, 'If you'd been frank with us, you'd have saved your wife a lot of distress. From her description of your injuries, it's inconceivable these men were burglars.'

'Well they were,' Brian said obstinately.

'Now, you listen to me!' Millson said fiercely. 'I've seen dozens of burglaries and investigated all kinds of attacks. This was a revenge attack. It was carried out by professionals and they don't make mistakes. If you don't come out with the truth you'll be answering any further questions down at the police station!'

Brian Hall gazed at him as though mesmerised. Then he

shrugged his shoulders. 'You're quite right. They weren't burglars,' he said, and went on to explain the attack had been Harry Weston's revenge for planting a bug in his computer system.

'So you knew Weston was behind it from the start?'

'Yes.'

'Why didn't you report it? Your wife tells me you wouldn't let her call the police or even an ambulance.'

Hall shrugged. 'I wasn't prepared to go through the hassle of statements and police inquiries when it was obviously impossible to prove Weston was responsible for it.'

'Or perhaps you didn't want any record of it in police files,' Millson suggested.

'I don't understand.'

'Don't play dumb with me,' Millson said sharply. 'You know very well we wouldn't have discovered your connection with the dead man if these photos hadn't come to light. Why didn't you tell us straight away?'

'I didn't want to become a suspect for his murder,' Brian said mildly. 'I see now that was a mistake.'

'A mistake? More like deliberate withholding of information,' Millson said severely. 'What else haven't you told us?'

'Nothing. There's nothing to tell. I caused Weston a lot of trouble and he had his revenge. End of story.'

'I see. You were badly beaten, your house trashed, your wife insulted, and you turned the other cheek.' Millson's tone was heavy with sarcasm. 'I'll tell you what I think, Mr Hall. I think you were seething with rage and wanted to kill him for what he did.'

Brian's eyelids were twitching. 'Well, yes, I was upset and angry, of course, and I admit I felt like killing him. But now, someone else has killed him and I'm very glad he's dead.' He smiled at Millson.

164

The smug smile, and his cocksure manner, were too much for Millson. He gave Scobie a nod to continue the questioning before he lost his temper.

Scobie laid down his notebook. 'Where were you last Wednesday week between six and ten in the evening, Mr Hall?'

'Here at home,' Brian said confidently.

'With your wife?'

'No, she spent the day at her mother's in London. I picked her up from the station about nine thirty.'

'Colchester station?'

'Yes.'

'What time did you leave the house to pick her up?'

'It's about a quarter of an hour to the station from here so I would have left around nine fifteen.'

'And Mr Weston's house at Kelvedon is about twenty minutes drive away, I believe?'

'I suppose so.'

'We know now he was killed shortly before nine. You could have left here at, say, half eight, driven to Kelvedon, killed Weston and been back at Colchester station by nine thirty to meet your wife.'

'Yes, I probably could,' Brian said diffidently. 'But I didn't.'

Scobie picked up his notebook. 'What's the make and colour of your car, Mr Hall?'

'A Ford Focus. Silver.'

'And your wife's?'

'A powder-blue Mini.'

'Egotistical sod!' Millson yanked his seat belt aggressively.

'D'you think he's capable of murder, though?' Scobie asked.

'Oh, he's capable,' Millson said grimly. 'Don't let those

165

doggy eyes fool you. He didn't report the attack and the vandalism because he'd already decided to kill Weston. He knew he wouldn't get away with it if his name was linked with Weston's in a police report of violent assault. He'd be a suspect.'

He dropped Scobie outside Kathy Benson's flat in Tanniford. 'Leave the files with me, Norris,' he said, as Scobie reached in the car to retrieve his briefcase. 'I want to go through them again.'

At his own house, Millson took advantage of Dena's absence at a school disco to sit quietly with a large whisky and read all the notes and reports on the case. When he'd finished he considered his list of possible suspects. First, Harry Weston's wife, Yvonne. She hated him, profited from his death by gaining his half of the business, and was having an affair with Richard Layton.

Brian Hall. Weston had had him badly beaten up and his house trashed. The violence and damage had been appalling, yet Hall had refused to report it and his explanation for that was a lie.

Richard Layton. He'd been keen to acquire Weston's business, but he had plenty of money and would hardly commit murder to get it. However, Harry might have unearthed evidence that showed Layton was involved in the disappearance of Katrina Kovacs. Anything that tied Layton and his cousin to her death, like hiding her body, or faking her departure, would be motive enough for them to silence him.

Four possible suspects with motive, opportunity, and no reliable alibi, but no real evidence against any of them. Worse, he had no leads and the only ongoing inquiries would be in the neighbourhood of the Halls' bungalow to see if anyone had information on the movements of their cars the night of the murder.

Millson sighed and poured another whisky. He picked up Hersham Associates' report on Richard Layton and began re-reading Rory Grant's account of his interview with Julia Dean.

When Millson reached his office next morning a clerk from the Incident Room was waiting to see him. In the process of tidying the room and sorting the accumulation of scraps of paper and envelopes, he'd come across the envelope stamped 'Hersham Associates' that had contained the report sent to Harry Weston. As with all envelopes, he opened it fully to make sure it was empty before throwing it away.

'I'm not sure if this was intended to be thrown away, or if it was overlooked, sir,' he said, tactfully, handing Millson a crumpled piece of paper. 'It was crunched up in the bottom of the envelope.'

Millson frowned over the page of notepaper. All that was written on it was a line of symbols. They were mainly right angles and three-sided squares, some upside down and side-ways, and some with dots in the middle.

'Thank you. I haven't the foggiest idea what it is, or whether it's of any significance, but you did right to bring it to me.'

Millson followed the clerk out and went next door to Scobie. 'Have a look at this, Norris.'

Scobie glanced at the sheet of notepaper. 'Looks like some kind of code. What is it?'

'It was in the envelope in Weston's safe containing Hersham Associates' report on Richard Layton.'

'Could be anything then. Safe combination, perhaps?' Scobie suggested.

'Maybe. Fax a copy to the Forensic Lab at Huntingdon and see what they make of it. After that we're going to Ridgewell to see Julia Dean.'

Last night, reading Rory Grant's meticulous notes and almost verbatim report of his interview with Julia Dean, Millson realised she was the one person who might hold further information that could provide a lead on the case.

Nineteen

At Ridgewell, Millson and Scobie identified themselves to the receptionist and said they wanted to speak to Mrs Julia Dean. She asked them to wait and picked up the phone. A minute or two later, a grey-haired man in a white coat, name-tag dangling from the breast pocket, came along the corridor behind her and approached them.

'I'm Doctor Cassell, Mrs Dean's doctor. Can I help you?'

'We really need to speak to Mrs Dean herself, doctor,' Millson said. 'We're investigating a murder.'

'I see.' Dr Cassell pursed his lips. 'You'd better come to my office then.'

They followed him along the corridor and up a flight of stairs to a room on the first floor. He sat down at a desk and waved them to seats. 'Unfortunately, Mrs Dean is very disturbed at the moment. She's not in a fit state to be interviewed and I doubt you would get much sense from her anyway.'

'How long has she been like this?' Millson asked.

'It happened about two weeks ago. Normally, she's a model patient. Calm . . . cheerful . . . lucid much of the time. This sudden increase in agitation was a complete surprise to us.'

'Do you know what caused it?'

'Only that what seems to be upsetting her is she believes someone entered her room and stole her treasure.'

'What is this treasure?'

Dr Cassell sat back and put the tips of his fingers together. 'Ah, well there's the problem. She still seems to have everything she brought with her when she was admitted. Whatever it is, she's convinced now it's been taken she'll be locked up behind bars again. By the way, we don't put patients behind bars here, not even in the secure wing.'

Bells began ringing in Millson's head. *The annexe at Hawkhills . . . Rory Grant's interview . . .* 'Could this treasure be a red exercise book, doctor?'

Doctor Cassell's jaw dropped. 'Good heavens! Yes. We assumed Julia had thrown it away. That's brilliant, Chief Inspector. How on earth did you deduce that?'

'With a bit of help from another source,' Millson said. 'Did Mrs Dean have any visitors recently?'

'Only the solicitors who call regularly. Without appointment.' He gave a thin smile. 'I think it's to check we're not ill-treating her. No one else, though. Mind you,' he went on. 'It wouldn't be difficult for someone to visit her without our knowledge. The rooms do have patients' names on the doors, and we don't have locked doors and security checks in this wing.' He looked at Millson. 'But who would steal a red exercise book?'

'I don't know,' Millson said. But he had a very good idea. 'Well, thank you, Doctor Cassell, you've been a great help. I'd be glad if you didn't mention our visit to anyone, particularly not to Mrs Dean's family.'

Dr Cassell nodded. 'D'you think it would ease her distress if we told her we know it's her red book that's missing?'

'It might if you also tell her she's safe here and you won't let her go back to Hawkhills.'

As they walked down the stairs Scobie said enthusiastically, 'You knocked him out with that brilliant deduction about the red book.'

'There was nothing brilliant about it, Norris. Plain old-fashioned police work. I went through everything we'd got last night, including the inquiry agent's report of his interview with Julia Dean. He was very observant.'

'What is this red book then?'

'I'm only guessing, but I think it was Katrina's diary and she probably used to hide it. Then, years later, Julia Dean found it during the time she was kept locked in the annexe before being committed. She'd be less deranged then than she is now and, realising what it was, she hung on to it, hoping perhaps to bargain with it for her release.'

'So, who took it?'

'Harry Weston, almost certainly. From the inquiry agent's report, he thought the notebook might contain dirt on the Laytons. He came down here, got into her room without being spotted, as Doctor Cassell suspected, and stole it.'

'And where's the notebook now?'

'The killer has it, of course. That's why Harry was murdered. To prevent him revealing what's in it.'

Soon after they returned to Colchester Millson had a call from Huntingdon laboratory's cryptologist.

'This is Pigpen code,' Jagelman said. 'It's been around since the seventeen hundreds when the Freemasons used it to keep their records private. In recent years it was mostly used by schoolchildren to keep the naughty bits in their diaries secret from their mums and dads. These days they probably don't even keep diaries.'

'Thanks for the history, but what does it say?'

'I can't tell you without more of it. There are only thirty characters here.'

'That's all we have.'

'Oh, dear.' Jagelman gave a sigh. 'Even with a simple code like this I need more than that to do a frequency test. Presumably this is connected with a case you're working on else you wouldn't have sent it to us?'

'Yes, a murder inquiry.'

'Then you might be able to work it out yourself more easily than I could.'

'You're joking.'

'Far from it. I notice there are five different characters standing alone in this piece of coding. These won't be figures because figures are written in clear in Pigpen code. Now, the only single characters in narrative are an I and an A, so one or more of these five must be an initial. So, if this coding *is* connected with your inquiry the initials could refer to people in the case. And with your knowledge of whose initials these might be, and if I explain Pigpen code to you, there's every chance you can work out what this says. Ever played noughts and crosses?'

'I did as a kid.'

'Right. Get yourself paper and pencil and draw a noughts and crosses frame for me.'

Millson reached for a sheet of paper and drew on it. 'Done.'

'Now, instead of noughts or crosses, enter the alphabet in the frame starting at the top left and putting two letters in each space. AB in the first, CD in the second and so on.'

Obediently, Millson filled in the frame. 'That takes me to R,' he said.

'OK. Now draw a large X and continue the alphabet, again putting two letters in each quadrant of the X, starting in the top segment with ST and proceeding clockwise. You'll find this exactly takes the rest of the alphabet.'

Millson did as instructed. 'OK.'

'You now have an angular shaped symbol for every two letters of the alphabet, a right angle for E and F, a square for I and J, for instance. In encoding, the second of the two letters is indicated by a dot placed in the middle of the right angle, square or whatever. D'you see that these shapes correspond with those on your piece of paper? Simple, isn't it?'

'Yes, and now you're going to tell me why it isn't simple to decode,' Millson said sourly.

'Oh, it's simple, but it's laborious,' Jagelman said cheerfully. 'You see, even a dim schoolchild knows better than to start the alphabet in the top left of the frame, because an equally dim parent could easily decode what they wrote. So, they begin the alphabet somewhere else and carry on round the frame to where it started.

'But you're going to tell me how to get round that, I trust.'

'Yes. The obvious way is to write out twenty-six frames starting the alphabet in every possible position, then slog through them to find which version makes sense of your piece of code. A quicker way for you is to write out the frames that bring the initial of one of your suspects or witnesses to correspond with a symbol standing alone in your piece of code. Of course, if that doesn't work you'll have to slog through all twenty-six possibilities. But in that case it probably means the coding has nothing at all to do with your inquiry.'

At Hawkhills that evening Rick and Drusilla Layton were seated either side of the Inglenook fireplace waiting for Amy to bring the after-dinner coffee.

Drusilla said languidly, 'Saturday tomorrow. Shall we have a lazy day on *Moon Rider*?'

'Yes, OK. Forecast's good.' He finished his liqueur and put down the glass. 'Dru, darling . . .' He hesitated. 'Don't you think the time has come . . .' – he groped for words – '. . . to start living our own lives?'

Her head reared like an animal scenting danger. With an effort she kept her voice steady. 'What's brought this on all of a sudden?'

He avoided her eyes. 'I'm in love with Elaine.'

She stiffened. 'It'll pass. It always does.'

'Not this time.' He rose and went to the French windows, looking out into the twilight. 'It's the real thing, Dru. I want to marry her.'

Drusilla went cold with fear. 'She's married already.'

'It's a hopeless marriage. She's going to leave Brian and get a divorce.'

She jumped up and began pacing restlessly back and forth. 'I see. You've already discussed it, have you? Without telling me?' Her eyes glinted. 'You can't do this, Rick. You can't leave me.' Her voice rose. 'Have you forgotten what we did with Katrina?'

She stopped pacing and flung the words across the room at him. '*We did it for us, Rick! US!*' she screamed.

There was a sound behind her. She spun round. Amy stood in the doorway holding a tray of coffee, her eyes wide with shock.

Drusilla stepped forward quickly. How much had the girl heard? Forcing a smile she said, 'Thank you, Amy, I'll take that.'

Amy handed her the tray then turned and hurried out.

Drusilla carried the tray to a coffee table. Rick turned back from the window and returned to his chair. 'Please don't take it so hard, Dru,' he begged. 'We'd still be friends.'

Her lip curled. 'When were we ever just friends? In the nursery?' She went and stood over him, putting a hand on his shoulder. 'You don't have to marry her, Rick. I won't mind. Have I ever minded your affairs?'

'This is not an affair.'

'But we belong to each other.' She dropped to her knees in front of him. 'Please, darling . . . don't do this to me.' She clutched his hands.

He looked away from her. She released his hands and sank forward, laying her head in his lap. 'You really mean it, don't you, Rick?' she said in a subdued voice.

'Yes.' He stroked her hair. 'It's best for both of us if we separate, my love.'

'Is it? You don't know what this will do to me.' She was quiet for a while. 'Have you told her about us?' Her voice was muffled.

'No, of course not. Dru, you wouldn't . . .'

She lifted a face streaked with tears. 'No, of course I wouldn't.'

Later she said, 'I suppose our day out on *Moon Rider* is off now?'

'No, of course not. Why should it be?'

She sighed. 'Oh, good.'

Amy tossed restlessly, disturbed by frightening dreams. She awoke with a start and switched on the bedside light. Drusilla was standing at the foot of her bed.

Drusilla had come into her room at night before. Usually she would sit on the bed, asking Amy what sort of a day she'd had, and talk about housekeeping problems. There would be the occasional caress, touching Amy's hair or face – never anything Amy felt she could object to. The visits lasted about ten minutes and then Drusilla would kiss her goodnight and leave.

Tonight was different. There was no warmth in Drusilla's eyes. They were cold and hard.

'Why did you look frightened this evening when you ran out of the lounge?' she asked.

Amy said quickly. 'Because you were shouting.'

'What was I shouting?'

'I don't know. I didn't hear.'

Drusilla sat down on the bed. 'Don't be silly, you must have heard what I said.'

'No . . . no, really I didn't, Drusilla.'

'Why were you frightened then?'

'Because you were quarrelling. You and Rick never quarrel.'

Drusilla moved closer. Her eyes seemed enormous as they stared into Amy's. 'You're lying!'

'No, I'm not,' Amy said, dropping her eyes.

Drusilla stood up, her face expressionless. 'Very well, my pet.' She bent and tucked the duvet around Amy, then kissed her cheek. 'Go to sleep now.'

At the door she turned and looked back, her eyes smudged shadows in a white face. The white face smiled sadly. She turned and walked out, closing the door behind her. Seconds later, Amy heard the bolts on the door from the kitchen being rammed home.

She leapt out of bed and ran through the hallway to the door. 'Drusilla!' She pounded on the door. '*Drusilla!*' She fell to the floor with a sob. With bars on all the windows, she was imprisoned as securely as in a prison cell. Drusilla would be back. Amy was certain of that. And there was no bolt on the inside of the door.

Terrified, she scrambled to her feet and ran back to the bedroom. Dragging a chest of drawers out into the hall, she pushed it against the door. She went into the sitting-room and pulled the table and chairs out into the hall and piled them on top of the chest.

Then she went back to the bedroom and sat down to wait.

Twenty

I n the breakfast room at Hawkhills Rick asked, 'Where's Amy this morning, Dru?'

'In Colchester, I imagine. I gave her the day off as we're going to be out on *Moon Rider* all day.'

'Uh-huh.' He looked at his watch. 'I've got to call in the office first.' He stood up. 'We'll meet at the yacht club. OK?'

She watched his car drive away then went into the kitchen. As she approached the door to the annexe the phone rang. She turned and lifted the kitchen extension. There was a mumble of disjointed words.

'*Granny?* Is that you?' she asked. 'Yes, this is Drusilla. Speak slowly.'

Millson was weary and frustrated when he arrived at his office next morning. Yesterday evening at home, he'd worked laboriously through different positions for starting the alphabet as Jagelman suggested and not found one that made sense of the line of code. He'd brought the remaining layouts to the office with him and put them in his desk drawer.

He continued working on them, taking one out and working on it surreptitiously then stuffing it back in his drawer if someone came in the room. He imagined the ribald comment if anyone saw him. 'Going in for a competition, sir?' The amusement in the incident room: 'DCI's gone bananas. He's playing noughts and crosses by himself!' And in his mind the thought that the piece of paper could turn out to be nothing to do with the case. Perhaps not even be connected with Harry Weston.

He'd begun on the third layout when he saw the first few characters were making sense. *R and D* . . . Revitalised, he pressed on.

There was a knock and a WPC entered. 'Not now! GO AWAY!' Millson shouted, and she hurriedly withdrew. Working furiously he finished decoding and read what he he'd written.

'Oh, my God,' he muttered. He stared at the words for a while. Then, putting the sheet of paper and the original line of code in his pocket, he went next door to Scobie.

'Let's go, Norris. I know why Katrina was killed,' he said.

Moon Rider slipped from her moorings in the deep water pool at the yacht club and purred quietly into the creek beyond with Rick Layton at the helm and Drusilla by his side. The elegant cruiser, and the couple on her bridge, attracted envious glances as they glided past the clubhouse.

Rick took the cruiser through the moorings in Foundry Creek and Walton Channel and past the vessels at anchor off Stone Point. Abeam of High Hill buoy he opened the throttles and *Moon Rider* rose in the water and planed over the calm sea towards Gunfleet Sands.

Rory Grant had phoned Hawkhills several times that morning. There was no answer and neither did the answer-phone cut in, which surprised him. He wanted to tell Amy about his new job and ask her to forgive him and if he could see her again.

John Hersham had been understanding and helpful when Rory told him he didn't want to work for him any longer.

'Well, you're not really cut out for the work we do here anyway, son,' Hersham said. 'You've got the appearance and the brain, but you're far too nice for this job. I'll give you a good reference.'

Rory had put on his best suit, had his hair cut, and presented himself at the offices of a local newspaper. He didn't get a job as a journalist, which he would have liked, but they did take him on as a cub reporter. He could hold his head up and face Amy again.

Now he was worried, though. He decided to drive over to Hawkhills and see why no one was answering the phone.

Millson and Scobie had given no warning they were coming and the German Shepherd dogs were roaming the garden of Constance Layton's cottage when they arrived. They waited at the gate until the barking brought Constance Layton to the door and she saw them. She called the dogs off and confined them in the rear garden.

'Not that again!' she said angrily when they were seated in her small front room and Millson told her he wasn't satisfied with her explanation of Katrina's departure from Hawkhills. 'My mother saw her go and there must be other witnesses too . . . at the station . . . on the train. You can't have tried hard enough to find them.'

'Oh, I accept that a woman looking like Katrina, and a man, left Hawkhills with Katrina's belongings that day, Mrs Layton. But that wasn't Katrina. That was your daughter, Drusilla, and her cousin Richard.'

'Have you gone completely mad, Chief Inspector?'

'No, and if you insist on maintaining this fiction, I'll have Drusilla and Richard lined up in an identity parade for the taxi driver to look at.'

It was a bluff. Millson had no intention of arranging an identity parade because there was no hope of Fred Parsons

179

picking them out. He saw Constance Layton's expression change, and pressed on.

'Katrina was already dead then, wasn't she? What happened, Mrs Layton? A quarrel? An accident perhaps?'

Constance Layton remained immobile, her face expressionless.

'Come on,' he urged. 'I know she's dead. You can't go on forever pretending she isn't. I have the evidence now. Tell us what happened.'

She turned her head and stared at him for a while. Then she shrugged. 'Very well.' Speaking carefully, as though choosing her words, she said, 'Katrina told me she'd seen Rick and Drusilla having sex and threatened to tell their fathers and the police because Dru was only fourteen. I begged her not to because of what it would do to all of us. She wouldn't listen. When I tried to reason with her she just became more and more stubborn and I lost my temper. I was so angry that she couldn't see the harm she would do, I picked up a hairbrush and hit her. I didn't hit her hard but she fell backwards and banged her head on an oak chest.' She raised her head and looked him in the face. 'It was an accident, Chief Inspector. I didn't intend to kill the girl, for heaven's sake.'

Constance Layton said she was appalled by what she'd done but afraid to call the police because they might think she'd done it deliberately. It wouldn't bring Katrina back, only cause a great deal of unhappiness and hurt to everyone. While she was wondering what to do, she said, Drusilla came into the room and found her standing over Katrina's body. When she explained what had happened, Drusilla pleaded with her not to call the police and suggested a way out.

'She and Rick pretended to be Katrina and a man leaving Hawkhills, and I picked them up later at Colchester and took them to the beach,' Constance told Millson. 'It was terribly wrong, but that's what we did.'

Scobie looked at Millson expecting a signal to formally caution Constance Layton. Millson frowned at him and shook his head.

'You almost make it sound believable, Mrs Layton,' he said. 'It's a very long way from the truth, though.'

'*What?*' She gaped at him.

There was no response when Rory Grant pressed the buzzer on the gate at Hawkhills. With growing unease he parked his car in the road and walked up the drive to the front door. He rang the bell and banged loudly with the knocker. When there was no answer he began walking round the building looking in the windows.

As he approached the barred windows of the annexe Amy saw him and jumped up, shouting and banging on the window. He gave her a thumbs-up sign and ran to the kitchen door. Within a minute or two he'd broken in, unbolted and unlocked the door to the annexe, and was holding a sobbing Amy in his arms.

'I don't understand,' Constance Layton said. 'What more do you want from me?'

'The truth,' Millson said.

'I've told you—' She stopped as the phone on the table beside her rang stridently. She picked it up.

Dr Cassell was apologetic. When Julia was admitted suffering from dementia, Constance Layton had insisted her mother shouldn't have access to a telephone in case she made upsetting calls to the family.

'I'm sorry, Mrs Layton, but I'm afraid your mother managed to elude the nurses this morning and phoned your daughter,' he told Constance on the phone. 'She must have asked her to come and see her because they saw Drusilla driving away from here a little while ago looking very upset. I thought I should let you know.'

Constance Layton put down the phone then picked it up again and began keying. 'Drusilla has been to see her grandmother in Ridgewell,' she told Millson. 'I must find her at once.'

When the phone rang at Hawkhills, Amy answered. 'No, Mrs Layton,' she said when Constance asked if Drusilla was there. 'She and Mr Rick have gone out on *Moon Rider*. Miss Drusilla locked me—' But the phone had gone dead.

The steward at the yacht club listened to the agitated voice vibrating the earpiece. '*Moon Rider* left the mooring about half an hour ago, Mrs Layton,' he said.

'My daughter's on board and I must speak to her! It's desperately important.'

'I'll call the coastguard for you,' the steward said. 'They'll make radio contact and then she'll be able to phone you ship-to-shore.'

'Thank you.' Constance put down the phone and faced Millson again.

'You've admitted killing Katrina,' Millson said. 'But where is her body?'

She hesitated then said, 'There are some gravel workings near Hawkhills, along the lane leading to Alresford Creek. On the other side of the lane there are some disused gravel pits. Some of them have filled with water and turned into quicksand. That's where I put her. The children weren't involved. I put her in the boot of the car and drove there alone.'

Scobie looked at Millson again. Surely he would charge her now?

Millson was about to question how she could handle Katrina's body unaided when the phone rang again.

It was the coastguard. The cruiser was lying at anchor about three miles off shore near the Medusa buoy, they told her. They'd radioed the vessel, using her call sign, but she was not responding and they assumed the radio was switched off. They would try to contact the nearest vessel.

When Constance put down the phone her face was drawn and haggard. 'The coastguard can't get an answer,' she told Millson. 'And I'm nearly out of my mind with worry. I can't answer questions until I've spoken to Drusilla, really I can't. Please, you must understand.'

Millson nodded, jerked his head at Scobie, and stood up. Scobie followed him out to the garden. 'What the hell's going on, George?'

'Later, Norris. Later. Wait until she's spoken to her daughter.'

Moon Rider lifted gently on the swell as she lay at anchor on the edge of Gunfleet Sands. Drusilla gazed out of the state-room window. 'D'you remember how we used to sail our dinghy out here when we were children, and play games on the sands, Rick?'

He slipped an arm round her shoulder. 'Yes, of course I do.'

She said quietly, 'We shan't be able to do this again.'

'Dru . . . don't,' he begged.

She turned to face him. 'Tell me you love me.'

He took her in his arms. 'You know I do.'

She lifted her face. 'Kiss me then.'

He bent his head, closing his eyes as their mouths met. The razor-edged seaman's knife went into his heart from below the ribcage. His eyes opened wide in shock.

'It's not because of Elaine or Katrina, my darling. It's . . .' She whispered the truth in his ear as his eyes glazed and he sagged against her. Gently, she lowered him to the floor.

183

Her face wet with tears, Drusilla laid the seaman's knife beside his body and went out on deck and up to the flying-bridge. She started the engines, engaged the electric windlass and hauled in the anchor. She set the grid compass for the Goldmer Gat and eased the throttles forward.

'Hallo,' said the coastguard who was keeping an eye on *Moon Rider's* blip on the radar screen. 'She's on the move again.'

When the depth sounder registered fifty metres, Drusilla reduced power until the cruiser was barely making way and switched to automatic pilot. She went below and opened the seacocks, then returned to the stateroom and picked up the knife. Clenching her teeth, she sliced open both wrists then lay down beside Rick's dead body, holding it close.

The cruiser moved slowly forward, the bilges filling and the hull sinking lower in the water until the engines flooded and stopped.

Moon Rider's bow dipped, the stern rose in the air and she dived to the bottom of the sea.

The coastguard watching the cruiser through his glasses swore. 'They've scuttled her!' He picked up the phone.

Constance Layton came out into the garden, her face ashen. 'It's all over,' she told Millson, her voice tremulous with emotion. 'Drusilla's killed herself and Rick too. You can—' She broke off and ran back indoors.

They followed her into the sitting-room. 'You've had a dreadful shock, Mrs Layton,' Millson said gently. 'I think you'd better just sit for a while and let Sergeant Scobie bring you a cup of tea. Or something else perhaps?'

'No, it's all right, thank you. I'd like to get this over quickly.'

'Very well. Tell me about Harry Weston then.'

Harry Weston had been disappointed to find Katrina's diary contained nothing of interest, just girlish chit-chat. Then he came to the last entry and the lines of code. Intrigued, he copied them out and took them to an expert who showed him how to decode them. It had taken Harry longer than Millson.

Constance Layton shuddered. 'A loathsome man. He phoned and said he had proof I killed Katrina. I said I didn't believe him and asked to see it. He told me to call the following night when his wife would be at the theatre. He showed me a red exercise book he'd stolen from my mother and said he wanted money for it. He wanted sex too. I was so disgusted I picked up a knife from the kitchen rack and went for him. Yes, I killed Harry Weston.'

'Not like that, you didn't,' Millson said. 'And that's not the reason you killed him. You brought the knife with you because you already knew what was in the diary . . . a secret Katrina found so shocking she used code to record it. The secret you killed Harry to prevent him revealing, and the secret your mother told Drusilla.'

Constance Layton was staring at him and listening, trance-like.

'Rick and Drusilla aren't cousins they're brother and sister,' Millson said. 'That's the secret that had to be kept at all costs, especially from them.'

There was a long silence. At last Constance said wearily, 'Yes, Drusilla wasn't my husband's child, she was Lionel's, his brother. Rick's father. I had an affair with him. No one knew she was Lionel's, not even Lionel himself. She's been sleeping with her own brother all these years. When my mother told her, it sent Drusilla over the edge. She couldn't go on living.'

'And when Katrina discovered they were having sex and overheard you telling your mother their true relationship she threatened to tell the police if you didn't put a stop to it and tell Rick and Drusilla,' Millson said.

'How could I tell them? It would have torn the family apart, wrecked Lionel's marriage and mine, and destroyed them both. I told Katrina it was just a teenage crush they would grow out of and begged her not to tell anyone, but she wouldn't listen. They didn't grow out of it, of course, they just grew closer. As the years past, and they were happy together, I became resigned to the situation.' She fell silent, looking away from her.

'A last question,' Millson said. 'You couldn't have carried Katrina's body to the gravel pit on your own. Who helped you?'

'Drusilla and Rick.'

'Thank you.' Millson nodded to Scobie.

Scobie stood up and began the arrest proceedings.